Sorcerer's Legacy

Wiccan Haus Book 12

By
Carolyn Spear

Copyright © 2016 by Carolyn Spear
ISBN: 978-1-68361-115-8
Cover art by Fiona Jayde

Published by
Decadent Publishing Company, LLC

Look for us online at:
www.decadentpublishing.com

Welcome to the Wiccan Haus

Something wiccan this way comes to a mystical mysterious island where authors get to play and bring their love stories to life. At the Wiccan Haus you will meet Rekkus, Cyrus, Sage, Sarka, Cemil and Myron, all of whom return in most if not all the stories. Yes each one will eventually get their HEA as well.

We hope you enjoy the stories from all the authors and return time and again to keep up with the staff and meet new characters along the way. But fear not if this is your first or twenty-first story each book stands on its own.

~A Note from the Author~

Welcome to Wiccan Haus. I know you'll love this series as much as I do. It is a world of possibilities, an escape from our daily realities. An island with shifters, witches, and all manner of paranormal beings, there's mystery and magic around every bend, in each encounter.

I'm Carolyn Spear, mother of two sweet girls and wife of one fabulous husband. Reading, gardening and exploring are my passions. I don't really "write" but rather channel my characters' stories to share with others. A strange combination of small town girl, travel enthusiast and geek, I am thrilled to be a part of the shared world of the Wiccan Haus.

For Becca's personality, I channeled my inner child. I still believe in magic and knights in shining armor. She gets a little more than she bargains for at Wiccan Haus. Wizards and werewolves and vampires, oh my! Ian Branson is an older than usual hero, but I like my heroes a little more experienced. A little uptight and a little supercilious, he is surprised at the feral passion Becca unlocks in him. He has to deal with all the emotions he keeps under lock and key to function. I think he exemplifies many of us who function more than live. And it's a Merlin-inspired tale, who I've always felt got a raw deal at the end of his life so I wrote him a different ending.

I hope you'll enjoy this story as much I did in telling it. I'd love to hear your comments! You can contact me at carolynspear.romance@gmail.com.

Dedication

For my fabulous, supportive husband who supports my writing addiction with chocolate and coffee. Thank you so very much.

Chapter One

*R*ank has its privileges.
Ian Branson bit back an impatient curse. Not even the cleansing sea air soothed his ragged nerves.

The ferry shuttling the dozen humans to the island chugged forward in the soupy fog at a snail's pace. The rain dripped down with irritating consistency like a clock's second hand ticking in slow motion. He glanced at the rest of the passengers. One poor sap had lost his lunch before they'd even left the safety of the Maine harbor, though the others appeared made of sterner stuff. Maybe they were native Mainers.

Sure, rank had its privileges.

He never pulled rank. This time was different. He needed anonymity. After contacting Wiccan Haus for a well-deserved impromptu vacation, the Rowan siblings had granted his request to accompany the human guests on the ferry.

If he had traveled with the paranormal guests through the high security portal, someone would have recognized him at the main portal station. Being the Syndicate's chairman of R & R—Rules and Regulations on the Lawful Use of Magick and Innate Powers—meant enemies and allies alike knew his face. While he parlayed his position—for once—to secure special treatment, he preferred to be just Ian on this retreat.

Who am I kidding? This is no retreat. This is a bloody intervention.

He was a basket case.

He needed to get away like he needed his next breath. Focusing on work was next to impossible. His heart demanded revenge on those who had attacked his son at his school.

Allan was safe—thank the gods and his bodyguard Trevor Greene—but innocent women and children had been slaughtered. The damn Mundus Novus, the latest and nastiest of the rebel para factions, had kidnapped Allan's teacher, Cassidy Sinclair, and Dana, the pregnant wife of Wiccan Haus's head of security, Rekkus. Not all paras followed the Wiccan rede of *an it harm none*, much less more structured laws.

Safety was an illusion.

He ran his hand through his hair then pushed his fingertips into his throbbing temple.

Darkness threatened his control and his sanity. He should be filled with anticipation over being surrounded by magick, free to release the sorcerer he'd hidden under suits and ties. Instead, the minutes ticked by in slow motion. He didn't care to socialize with any of the other passengers, not until he regained his balance.

To pull his thoughts from the dark shadows of

his mind, he idly perused the guests near him. Two men, apparently involved from the joined hands and ease of nonverbal communication, leaned on the railing closer to the bow. An older woman smiled easily at a younger woman—probably her daughter or niece—who pointed to the island rising from the sea like a siren beckoning them with her song.

A good sign, waxing poetic. A hopeful sign.

The hairs on the back of his neck stood up. Someone watched him. He didn't trust his instincts to tell him if the person posed a threat. Right now everyone he met posed a threat. He stretched his arms up and worked the real kinks out of his neck while using the movements to camouflage looking around.

There.

For a split second, he caught the curious stare of the pretty redhead on the padded bench in front of the wheelhouse. Her hazel eyes widened and her mouth fell open in a small gasp at being caught observing him. A rosy blush spread quickly from the low neck of her clingy royal-blue sweater to her red roots. Probably Irish heritage.

Maybe simple female appreciation. Maybe something more sinister.

His gaze settled on a cameo above just a peek of cleavage. He restrained an unexplainable tidal wave of lust and attraction. Never had he experienced such a strong first reaction to a female. For a moment, he yearned to go to her, longed to touch her. He inhaled the scent of lavender mixed with salt from the rolling seas. Getting involved with a woman was the last thing he needed. At least right now.

Female company would be a good reward for regaining his balance. Hmm. Possibilities....

Ignore him. You have more pressing matters.

Becca Jones sighed as she forced her attention back to the open diary in her hands. Worn from years of use with its first owner, the book written in a strange tongue refused to reveal any pertinent information. The ruby ring she'd discovered in her grandmother's safety deposit box rotated freely on her middle finger as she nervously played with it. The letter with it said it had belonged to her father.

Who was her father?

If only the diary provided more details. Her late mother had written about everything but her father—friends, parties, homework even, for heaven's sake. Her mother had conceived her at the tender age of seventeen and been killed in a car accident when Becca was just a toddler.

I wished I'd known her. Am I like her in temperament or personality?

She didn't look like her; pictures showed a young, petite Lisa Jones with light-blonde hair. Becca's was auburn. Her grandmother Helen refused to talk much about her, said it hurt too much. When her grandmother died a few months ago, she'd inherited everything, including the diary and another book she needed to translate. Instead of the information she craved about her parents, more questions swirled in her head.

Answers to her past inspired this hastily planned trip. How she'd get them or why this place drew her, she didn't know. Wiccan Haus had a reputation for healing and she needed that, too. The hole in her heart left by the loss of her mother and never knowing her father had widened to a chasm with the death of her last living relative.

She was the last on her mother's side. Did she have family on her father's side? Would they want to know her?

The change in the rumbling motor's timbre pulled her out of her thoughts. People around her gathered their belongings, restless to get on with their holiday. They obviously had a clear purpose, a clear sense of self. She, on the other hand, had never been at such loose ends.

Who am I?

She rubbed her grandmother's cameo for comfort.

Mother, help me find what I'm looking for. Strangely, though she didn't remember her mother, she'd always spoken to her, felt her presence.

She grabbed her heavy leather backpack and began to sling it over her shoulder. It snagged on something. With an absent tug, she focused on the queue developing near the bow.

"Let me help you with that."

Her heart leaped in her chest as she swung to see the owner of the smooth, deep voice. Her gaze collided with the man who'd caught her studying him before. Face-to-face he appeared older than she'd expected from her first impression of his lean physique. His soft green eyes contrasted with the stern set of his mouth, both framed by a few fine lines of age. Longish dark-brown hair shot through with generous silver waved freely about his face in the stiff breeze.

She shook herself out of her stupor when he cocked an eyebrow.

I'm staring. Again.

Suppressing the desire to fan her heated face, she nodded. *I'm an idiot. A blithering idiot.*

After easily hoisting her bag over his shoulder, he waited wordlessly for her to join the line.

Why didn't I smile and introduce myself? That would have been polite. He's just being polite, and I probably won't see him during the week we're here. And I am talking to myself instead of conversing with another human being.

Only not so courteous as to introduce himself. Or ask to help her. He'd offered more as a foregone conclusion. Dressed in a brown tweed blazer over russet tailored slacks, he exuded a certain upper class confidence she lacked.

Perhaps unearthing her past would help her discover who she really was and illuminate a path for the future. Give her a foundation to build her own self-esteem.

The crowd of them, thirteen she counted, meandered off the boat in a crooked line to follow the winding path to Wiccan Haus.

Like cattle.

Nervous laughter bubbled out and she quickly slammed her hand over her mouth to stifle it.

"Hmm," said the handsome man with the deep voice. "Share, if you wouldn't mind. I could use some humor."

She didn't dare look at him. She'd just imagine his words coming out as moos. "I was thinking we resembled cattle being taken to market."

He snorted and chuckled. "I suppose we do."

6

Embarrassed, she refrained from further comment and hurried behind her fellow bovines. She always said what she thought and, when she said nothing, it was because her thoughts wouldn't be appreciated or appropriate. Her imagination worked overtime and her mouth continually got her in trouble.

Even now, the Tudor house before her rose from the ground three stories like Jack's beanstalk. The huge edifice seemed out of place on this mysterious island in the middle of the mist. In her whimsical mind's eye, a shimmering circle of witches dropped a gold seed on the ground, repeated a spell three times, and the imposing edifice rose fully built from the soil. Silliness, her grandmother would have said—had said—on many occasions at her wild imagination.

She'd learned to keep her thoughts inside. Books were her friends and, at times, her salvation. Adventure, love, and danger waited in every story and, when she needed one, a happy ending.

She hoped to find her happy ending here in this magical place.

Chapter Two

"Chairman."

Sage Rowan's mellifluous voice alerted him to her presence. He sighed. Normally his own empathic abilities, while self-dampened, allowed him a sort of proximity sensor. Right now, his uncontrolled abilities left him vulnerable.

The youngest Rowan sibling's serene beauty disguised a steely inner strength. Small in stature, slim and waiflike, Sage's sweet nature radiated despite the family's tragic history. He'd been the council member to push for granting the island to Cyrus Rowan in appreciation and compensation for his service to the Syndicate.

The gift would never repay the murder of three of his six siblings for that service.

Cyrus had needed a secure location to avoid the assassins looking to cash in on the bounty rebels had posted for his head. This magically protected fortress-cum-spa provided it.

Cyrus and Rekkus, their head of security,

prowled—an accurate description for the way the two huge men moved—toward the front desk. Both men, tall, dark, and deadly, strode with the lethal grace of stalking panthers. In Rekkus's case, a tiger.

He acknowledged them with a slight tilt of the head as Sage glided to him and clasped his hand in hers. Her perpetual clean scent of the herbs she nurtured engulfed him. Her other brother, Cemil, who matched her in pale coloring and calm temperament, stood relaxed at her side.

She's like an angel.

A knowing smile played at Cemil's lips.

I must be transparent.

The island's only absent major player was Sarka. He'd consulted with the eldest Rowan—a powerful alchemist—when dealing with cases relating to her specific craft and endured the lash of her acid tongue. She'd virtually made him beg to grant his last-minute request. Fine with him if she never appeared for the next week.

Myron, the Romani with a light-blue streak through her dark brown hair, worked the front desk, flipping her ever-present cards. Every time he'd visited, she'd been behind that desk. Did the woman never sleep? She arched a perfect black brow and tilted her head toward the card.

The queen of hearts. A trustworthy lover or mate. Can't be for me.

He glanced at Myron, wearing a "Trixie" nametag, who rewarded him with a bland look that revealed nothing.

Ian arched an eyebrow at Sage. "Sage—"

"Of course, Chairman. Myron," she said, her voice like a chime on a breeze, "the chairman's key, please."

The youngest Rowan oozed sweetness. He almost wished he were young enough to pursue her. Almost. It had been a very long time since he'd had much of a sex drive. She would be a diverting companion, not a lover. His latest clumsy attempt at acquiring an appropriate mate had proved him too old for the game. He should have known just because a woman fit the part, such as his son's teacher who already loved his child, didn't mean she wanted a marriage of convenience.

His gaze flicked to the redhead from the boat with the enchanting eyes and charming blush. She stood with a staff member by the third elevator. The one reserved for humans. He shoved away the surprisingly strong urge to follow her.

A holiday tryst wouldn't solve issues. Even if she were the first to stir his libido—like a tornado—he didn't need the distraction from this trip's purpose. He'd come here for one reason only. Regain his center and life. Get his control back. He dragged his attention back to the Rowans.

"Thank you. And please, don't call me Chairman this week. I'm just Ian Branson."

Cemil, eyebrow raised, seemed to understand his request to separate from his position for his time here. "Absolutely, Mr. Branson."

He snorted softly as he took the offered key from "Trixie." Grabbing his suitcase before anyone could accompany him to his room, he turned on his heel to make his escape. The sooner he started his relaxation and rehabilitation, the better.

Ignoring the glares of the humans herded by spa personnel into a loose line by the left elevator, he pushed the button for the middle lift. Each elevator only accessed one floor, keeping the paras and humans separate, with the right shaft reserved for Rowan siblings only.

He had the second elevator to himself. The portal for the paranormals did not open until the humans settled in for herb-induced naps. Sage prepared potpourri and candles specifically for each guest's needs and placed them in their rooms prior to arrival. He could wander the grounds undisturbed or relax in his room.

Alone.

His heart ached for Allan. He missed his little boy terribly. Coming home to his six-year-old son after a frustrating day dealing with the hidden world of the paranormal kept him sane. When Allan's arms wrapped around his neck and his head rested on his shoulder he understood why he had to serve the paranormal world. Protecting innocent lives, para and human, was his life's work. Centuries ago his ancestor Myrddin walked the razor's edge between the human and magical worlds. Ian must bear the same mantle of responsibility as his birthright and his curse. Until he had his steely control back, he was no good to anyone.

He fit the old-fashioned key into the lock and let himself into his room. No magnetic locks or electronic security at Wiccan Haus. Comfortable and spacious, the accommodations suited his needs. Naturally one of the resort's few cabins would have been preferable, but unavailable given his last-minute reservation.

He kicked off his shoes and stretched out on the fluffy down duvet. All he needed right now was a soft bed and solitude.

The stress and strain of the last months dragged his eyelids shut. Sage's herbs or his age catching up with him? Undeniable weariness pulled at his soul and instead of fighting the steady slumberous slide into darkness, for once he released the iron grip on his control and slept.

***

"You must safeguard our legacy."

Ian waded through waist-deep fog to the boulder where Myrddin stood. "I am doing my best, Grandfather."

The old man in long black robes shrugged his shoulder and jerked his hand to the side in dismissal. "You do nothing." Myrddin stroked his long white beard, spearing him with an intense stare. "You must find—"

Loud pounding reverberated, jarring him awake. Jerked from the dream, he rose and ran a hand impatiently through his hair as he strode to the door. Yanking it open, he faced a stone-faced Rekkus.

"Mr. Branson, it is time for dinner." From the curl of the big man's lip, apparently he didn't relish the responsibility of retrieving him.

Ian swallowed the frustration at the loss of Myrddin's message in the dream so he could force a courteous response. "Thank you, Rekkus. I appreciate you taking the time to personally come to my door."

Again, the man's lip curled as he imagined it did in his weretiger form.

"We go door-to-door waking the humans. I didn't imagine we'd have to wake you, too." Perhaps an insinuation he was old or weak like a human?

Ian choked back his outrage and said through gritted teeth, "Thank you all the same." He shut the door without another word.

Questions raced through his head. What did Myrddin expect him to do? He protected the family legacy—both humans and paras—as the great wizard's descendants had always done. What more could he do?

After shaving as quickly as he dared with a safety razor, he changed his clothes and headed down to dinner. He hoped to avoid dining with anyone this first evening. Without absolute control, he'd never make it through a meal at a tableful of vamps.

***

"Excuse me." Becca spoke softly, hating to bother the woman at the front desk.

The pretty gypsy woman looked up from the cards she shuffled. She laid down five cards in a row before replying.

"Yes, Becca. How may I help you?"

Becca blinked, surprised. Was the woman psychic? She chuckled, not bold enough to ask her burning questions. Yet. "Would you please tell me how to get to the library?"

With an enigmatic smile that rivaled the Mona Lisa's, the woman pointed. "Opposite the dining room; follow the hallway to the end. You should be in the dining room. Guests are expected to take evening meals there, you know."

"Oh, yes. I stepped out to powder my nose and thought I'd scope out the library while I was at it. I'm a librarian." Becca squinted at her nametag then raised her eyebrow. At check-in she had been Trixie. Now her nametag read "Bryce."

"Oh. Sorry, Becca. I'm Myron." The woman smiled at Becca.

Becca grinned and relaxed. "Nice to meet you, Myron. And thanks."

More at ease, she followed Myron's directions.

On the way, she peeked into the dining room to see if the handsome gentleman from the ferry had arrived for dinner yet. At a table on the side opposite where she had been seated was the man who'd inspired her fanciful heart to wonder at the possibilities. With him sat a perfect but very pale couple.

She cringed at the utter boredom on his face.

He glanced up, catching her staring again.

She quickly darted away, determined to find the library before he started to think she was stalking him, before the staff herded her back to the dining room.

Down a pale-yellow hallway, a set of imposing double wood doors guarded a room beyond. Her pulse fluttered. Such grand doors must protect a wondrous collection.

Like entering a sacred place, she slowly pushed one of the doors to slip inside. Libraries were her temples. Knowledge equaled power—the power to inform, inspire, persuade. Books had the ability to transport her to another place and time. Characters were as real as the people who walked the solid earth around her. In awe, she gazed at the vaulted ceilings, covered in gilded planking. She pushed the door closed, wanting to savor the moment in privacy.

The scent of rich leather and aging parchment drew her toward the books on the shelves. Wonder mingled with awe as she craned her neck to see the upper bookshelves, giggling with anticipation at climbing to the top on the built-in sliding ladder.

Almost giddy with excitement at the treasure of knowledge locked in the books, she traced her fingers over the bindings.

Where to start? This library's size made a quick search impossible. There were only a few minutes before the yoga class began. She quickly dismissed the classics and tomes of philosophy. Many she'd read. Wonderful first editions abounded but didn't assist her.

"Help me, Mother," she whispered and rubbed the cameo at her neck gently.

Her fingers tingled as she touched one book and she leaned closer to read the title. *Black Book of Carmarthen*. The cracked leather binding on the manuscript showed repeated use. This volume had been someone's well-loved possession at some point.

"Go ahead, take a look."

She jerked and squealed as she spun on her heel.

A tall, dark man leaned in the open doorway. With a formidable presence on his expressionless face and his squinting, assessing gaze, he intimidated her. He pushed off the doorframe and strolled to her. As he walked, he slowly stripped off the glove from his right hand. His gaze kept her frozen in place. What would he do? Should she run? Would anyone hear her if she screamed?

The stranger stopped a few feet from her and his mouth lifted at one corner in a slight lopsided smile.

She released the breath she wasn't aware she'd been holding.

"I hope I didn't scare you." He offered his right hand. "I'm Cyrus Rowan. One of the owners."

She clasped his hand, shaking it with false confidence and smiling back at him. "I'm Becca Jones. Librarian."

He held her hand for a moment longer, staring at her. He cocked his head as if she were a puzzle then released her.

"Becca Jones," he repeated, one dark eyebrow raised. "Much more than a librarian, Becca." He reached past her to retrieve the book that had caught her interest. "Here. May you find the answers you seek." He handed her the book and walked out.

What the hell?

Why had Cyrus Rowan, owner of Wiccan Haus, lent her a priceless text without blinking an eye?

After glancing at her watch, she hurried out of the library with the ancient book pressed to her chest like the treasure it was.

***

Kill me now.

Ian stretched his arms over his head while gauging the yoga instructor, Trixie. Young, buff, and sexy, she exuded a serenity gained from years of yoga. She smiled at him. He smiled in response, irritated the tall, ethereal beauty didn't inspire the same instant lust the redhead did.

Becca had stopped by the dining room archway to see him. Not to talk to him, just to see him. She'd blushed when he caught her staring, and he'd smiled the rest of the meal despite being stuck with the self-absorbed vamps.

He scowled now.

There could be nothing between them. His responsibilities to humans and paras to maintain a delicate balance through a strict code of ethics and behavior rose above his baser needs. Hell, he couldn't even control his own abilities right now.

Soft music drifted on the air, rich with birdsong and Celtic fiddle. Once he'd practiced yoga daily to compensate for the constant onslaught of others' feelings. Already, his mind released, his muscles relaxed. He'd avoided the mental quiet of yoga; he didn't want to be alone with his thoughts. Meditation made it too easy to lose himself in anger, anxiety, and grief.

He settled on his mat, adjusting his shorts for propriety. Trixie eased down on her mat, facing him, and folded herself into the traditional lotus pose.

What was she waiting for?

Being irritated certainly wasn't the right frame of mind to practice yoga so he closed his eyes, inhaled, and counted to ten. He'd avoided yoga since his wife's death, preferring the pure mind-numbing physical exhaustion running and kickboxing afforded to drain his tension. Yoga allowed too much time in his own head, but he came here for healing so he had to trust the Rowans and their staff knew what they were doing.

He exhaled slowly, determined to make the best of this experience, and opened his eyes.

Legs. And pretty coral-painted toes.

He squeezed his eyes shut. Was it really so much to hope for a private session? When he inhaled, the scent of vanilla and lavender filled his head.

Her.

He ground his teeth to keep the curses swirling in his brain from escaping out his mouth.

Is nothing sacred? he silently asked the gods, casting his gaze skyward.

"Namaste. Welcome. I'm Trixie."

He averted his eyes as the copper-haired woman sank to her mat and crossed her legs in lotus, mirroring the instructor. By the gods, how could he endure an entire session looking at her and maintain his sanity?

She stuttered a bit, revealing her nervousness. "I'm Becca."

"Nice to meet you, Becca."

Two sets of eyes stared at him expectantly.

"I'm Ian."

Wow, socialize much, idiot?

Trixie wrinkled her brow for a moment. She must have expected more from him as well.

"Okay. This first evening we're only working on breathing and stilling our minds. Just a short session. Tomorrow we move up in intensity in body and mind. There are towels and water in the corner. Take what you need." She pointed to the mini-fridge at the far end of the room next to the table laden with perfectly rolled towels. "And if you need a block to aid in some positions, we have those, too."

He glanced at Becca who filled out a pair of black yoga pants and tight emerald-green tank top to perfection.

Damn.

He folded his legs into what his son called "crisscross apple sauce" and pulled images of anything cold into his mind. Icebergs, igloos, Popsicles. Why, oh why, did his libido have to come roaring back to life on this trip? *Becca*, his inner voice said, taunting him. He'd get through this session and make sure they didn't have a lesson together again.

The fates have a plan. Forget their plan. He had free will and he would not get involved with this woman.

"Ian?"

He shook his head. *Ah, hell.* How long had she been talking to him? "Um. Yes?"

"Is everything all right?" Trixie asked, her brow furrowed in concern.

"Fine. Just fine. Let's breathe, shall we?"

He didn't dare glance at Becca, whose worry washed over him in inescapable, warm waves. Sweet, really, that she would worry about a complete stranger. He tried to close himself to her but couldn't. Concern mixed with an intense sexual awareness, an attraction. He shouldn't let her in but his balance was so off, he couldn't fend off her emotions, so he consciously opened himself.

God, such potent emotions. Exhilarating and intoxicating, those emotions poured into him. He savored the power.

So much anxiety, fear of anything new, her empathy for others she didn't know or understand. He recognized a potential as an empath from the deep well of compassion she hadn't tapped. Maybe didn't know how to access.

He shook his head clear. Such an anxious woman did not need a new problem. Nor did he.

The sound of someone clearing his throat from the door interrupted his thoughts. "Excuse me, Trixie. We need you in the lobby." The employee hesitated as he glanced at Becca for a second before turning his attention back to the instructor. "There's a problem with the feeding schedule."

Ian read between the coded lines.

Vamps. Damn blood suckers refuse to follow rules and everyone suffers.

Trixie rose effortlessly from the floor and turned to Ian. "Would you lead the meditation, Chair—I mean, Ian? I'll be right back." She followed the other staff member out the door without waiting for his answer.

With no other choice, he moved his mat to face Becca. He could do this. He inhaled deeply before raising his gaze to look at her.

"We can cancel." She sensed his hesitation. A dead man could sense his hesitation.

Pride forced him to straighten his spine. He folded his legs into lotus pose and glared at her. "No, we'll do this."

She rewarded him with a cocky smile, revealing a dimple. Determined not to be charmed by her, he deviated from Trixie's prescribed easy breathing lesson and led her in asanas more challenging to the mind and body. At least to his less limber body.

During the cool down, he realized Becca's anxiety had vanished during the session. Her emotions calmed, and he didn't need to erect a wall against her to function. Perhaps she *would* be a good yoga buddy.

The yoga was good for him, too, simultaneously energizing and relaxing his body and soothing his mind. If only her rear wasn't so perfect or her breasts so alluring. Her cleavage had enticed him every time she leaned toward him. He couldn't ignore the full bounty right in front of him.

She popped up, demonstrating his workout hadn't overly strained her, and sauntered to the fridge. As she returned, she tossed a bottle of water to him, along with a towel.

"Thanks, Ian. That was fun."

Fun? Damn. His body already ached in places he'd long forgotten existed, and she thought it was fun?

Running and kickboxing got him through his stressful days. His flexibility suffered as he would surely suffer tomorrow.

Unable to think of anything witty, he said, "Any time."

She wrinkled her brow. "Uh. Okay. Good night."

She swept out of the room, taking with her his peace of mind.

Chapter Three

Bleary eyed from a restless night of tossing and turning, Ian woke with an aching head and sore body. A glance out the window confirmed the weather reflected his mood. Huge drops pounded against the glass and dark clouds made the morning like night.

The whole bloody night thoughts of her—Becca—crowded his mind, blocking all his efforts to escape her spell. Damned attractive with her pinup body and shy glances, his body throbbed with undeniable need. He hadn't been this randy since he'd first been with Georgia Blankenship at the tender age of fifteen.

As he stripped off his pajama pants and pulled on a rugby shirt and khakis for the day, he glared at the ceiling and, in effect, the fates themselves.

You listen to me. I don't want her. I don't need her. I'll pick my own damn woman.

As he closed the door behind him, he was sure he heard the fates laughing.

In the dining room, Ian prepared his Irish

breakfast tea and selected one of the blueberry scones from the buffet table.

Reading would calm his frayed nerves this dreadful day, so he passed the few early risers and the front desk where Myron flipped her ubiquitous cards. Didn't that woman ever sleep?

With his breakfast balanced precariously in one hand, he levered open one of the heavy oak doors and slipped into the quiet of the library. As he inhaled the scent of old books and woodsmoke, the tension flowed out of his body. The fire crackled in the big stone fireplace, enticing him with its warmth and light. Flickering flames leapt up from the glowing logs. Fire was not his element—earth was— but fire entranced. Fire was passion, with the ability to create or destroy. Dangerous and seductive, fire could enchant a man to do what he shouldn't, like fine whiskey or a sensual woman.

Two leather armchairs faced the hearth. He sank into one, setting his tea and scone on the table next to him. Sipping his tea, he savored the first taste then the second. The wind rattled the window with a mighty gust and drew his attention.

In the window seat, huddled like a child beneath a throw, slept the very woman he wanted to avoid. He watched her a moment but she didn't move, so he finished his cooling tea and ate his scone.

Copper hair escaped her braid and waved about her face. Her pretty pink lips were parted slightly and her hands lay beneath her head, pressed together as if in prayer.

Allan sleeps like that.

Loneliness stole over him as he stared at the

lovely woman he had no business desiring. She must be at least ten years younger than he, and innocent. So innocent of the evils of the world, human and paranormal.

He let down his guard, allowing his emotions out of the box where he kept them locked down. Here, with Becca asleep, he could open his soul. Her emotions were muted while asleep. He could handle the vulnerability.

With his head back against the chair, he closed his eyes and blew out the remaining tension from his body. He stilled his mind.

Open. I free you.

Darkness crept over him as a black, smothering mist. Fear slammed into his gut and his heart like a physical blow. He fought it, pushed it back. Reinforced by desire for revenge, the dread caused by his son's attack ricocheted inside his body like a jagged bullet.

No. Not my son. Bastards. You leave my son alone. He's just a boy. I'll hunt you down and kill you.

Myrddin stood before him and the wicked mist slunk away. "Protect my legacy."

His shoulder jerked. Then again.

"Ian. Wake up. Ian."

He opened his eyes to gaze into Becca's very concerned face. Her quiet voice trembled slightly as though she were afraid of him. Why? She had nothing to fear from him. She dropped her hand from his shoulder and retreated a few feet.

"I'm sorry to wake you. It's just that you seemed agitated."

He scrubbed a hand over his face and found it

wet. *How can I explain crying? And why the hell does she appear afraid of me? Damn!*

She jumped, startled.

Did I say that aloud? By the gods, am I losing my fucking mind?

By the expression on her face—her eyes wide, her brows drawn together—she didn't understand what was going on either. Her anxiety pulsed from her in rolling waves that threatened to take him under.

Breathe. Control. Lock everything down again.

With every thought, she reacted with an arched brow or quirk of the mouth.

Use your words, Ian.

"Okay, Becca. Everything's fine." He tried his most soothing tone but from the increase in her emotional wave frequency, she didn't buy his load of horseshit.

"How can I hear your thoughts?" she asked, her voice trembling.

"I'm not sure and I don't like it, but we'll figure it out."

"I don't think I want to." She ran to the window seat and grabbed an ancient book and a rolled scroll. Her corduroy pants rubbed noisily as she hurried toward the door.

Ha. No way to outrun your problems. I know.

"Watch me try."

Shit, I hope there's a distance limit to her psychic ability. And a time limit.

"You're not the only one."

The door opened as she touched the handle, and Cemil stepped inside. Startled, she dropped the texts. Before she could retrieve them, Ian picked them up.

"This one is from this library. I gave it to them." He indicated the volume by lifting the *Black Book of Carmarthen*. The scroll in his hand vibrated slightly in his gentle grasp. "This one, however, belongs to my family. How did you get it?"

Her outrage exploded from her like a sledgehammer, sending him reeling back a couple of steps. He shook his head and retook his ground.

"I don't steal and I don't lie." She turned to Cemil, her nostrils flaring. "This is your magical island. Why the hell can I hear his thoughts?"

Cemil's eyebrow lifted as he glanced from Becca to Ian. "You share a connection."

"Really?" Sarcasm dripped from the two syllables. "I don't need to be psychic to know that."

Is she talking about the attraction between us?

Her head swiveled to gaze at Ian. "You're attracted to me?"

The corner of Cemil's mouth quirked up. Ian inhaled slowly to calm his racing thoughts. *The angrier she gets, the sexier. Shit. Not again.*

Before he could utter any intelligible words, she sputtered, "Oh, stop thinking of me that way, you idiot."

Cemil took Becca's hand and spoke softly to her. "Come with me. We'll see Sage to get you some soothing herbs. Ian, we'll talk later. Perhaps you should rest for a bit?" He closed the door behind him, leaving Ian alone.

What the hell is going on?

***

"Who does he think he is? Accusing me of stealing."

Becca paced as she ranted aloud. She awaited Sage in her herb garden, a paradise of sight and aroma. Rosemary vied with lavender to perfume the air, both doing so with perfect subtlety. Nasturtium in vibrant red and orange brightened a ledge next to the bench she'd perched on for a few minutes. She couldn't settle. She was too angry. No, angry was too mild a word; she was livid.

"He's a man with much responsibility, Becca."

She spun at the soft musical voice right behind her. What was up with these people scaring the jeepers out of a person? "Well, the scroll is mine."

"All right."

Her patient attitude irritated.

"It came down through my family."

"I understand."

"How can you? *I* don't."

Sage smiled then. "Life is a journey, not a destination."

"I've heard that before. Seen it on a bumper sticker."

"Yes, but in your case, you came here looking for specific answers to specific questions." She tilted her head toward the far end of the garden where Ian now stood.

How long had he been there? Had he witnessed her rantings? Good. Her pulse quickened due to fury, not attraction. The tightening of her belly and the flutter of her heart was from her rising blood pressure, not because she wanted to comb her fingers through his silvering hair.

"What if your questions lead you to something altogether different from what you expected?" Sage asked.

This was one crazy island. Why did they all speak in riddles? Couldn't anyone give her a straight answer? She found a clue in the Black Book and, without having a decent chance to study the book, they threw her down a rabbit hole to meet the Mad Hatter.

Sage stood, apparently waiting for an answer.... *Oh, yes. Finding something different from what I was originally looking for.*

"I don't know."

The waiflike blonde paused. "Fair enough. Let me suggest that the two people here who have clues are you and Ian." She began walking, and, with a slight tilt of her head, indicated for Becca to join her. "Ian is very knowledgeable in magick. I believe the two of you must follow the path together." Sage leaned in to whisper, "He is fluent in old Welsh. He will help you with the scroll."

To find her father's identity, Becca would cross deserts and oceans. She'd work with Ian to help figure out their connection, and he could help her translate the scroll. If she found her answers, Ian could have the parchment, though he didn't need to know it yet.

Sage stopped a few yards from the scowling man. He must have erected some sort of mental barrier; his thoughts no longer entwined with hers.

Ian extended his hand, though it seemed more demand than request. "Truce? We need each other for at least a little while, Becca. The sooner we work together to figure out the problem, the sooner we can fix it. And we'll translate the scroll."

What is his game?

"Don't look at me that way. With your brow all scrunched up and your nose wrinkled. I have some idea what I'm doing."

Becca shook his hand for the required two seconds then dropped it like a live grenade. His touch sent a delicious heat through her, the kind she only read about in books. Ian could not be her knight in shining armor, the hero of her story. He didn't even like her.

Dealing with her sudden psychic abilities ate away at her time to discover her father's name and origin. She straightened her back, drew up to her full five foot six, and looked him in the eye. The sooner she cut the connection with Ian, the sooner she could focus on her real objective.

"Let's do this."

***

Oh, God, what the hell am I doing?

Only a mad woman would accompany a man she barely knew to a secluded cove on the island. Ian had assured her they would not be interrupted. The Rowans reserved this area for their family's use and allowed them exclusive access.

His assurance did nothing to calm her jagged nerves.

Rapid-fire questions popped in her mind. *Why did this man think my scroll belonged to him? How did I suddenly begin hearing his thoughts and nobody else's? Why did Ian bring me here?*

She focused on the waves lapping gently

against the sand and the occasional gull's cry over the sea. Surrounded by rocks on three sides, the cove both sheltered and trapped. The sooner they got this over with, the better.

At least the weather cleared.

She hated not knowing what was going on. Books, she could count on. They never hurt her, never disappointed her. As a librarian, she controlled the collection and cared for the books. That she was a control freak like Ian slammed into her like a fist. She'd never considered she needed to control everything, but she never doubted her inner voice confirming.

The idea she was similar to Ian in any way was ridiculous. A giggle slipped out and he turned from setting the fire.

"At least you're not pissed off anymore."

She shifted on the blanket she'd spread on the sand to stare at him. "Who says I'm not?"

He just smiled and placed another piece of driftwood in the makeshift fire pit. "I can feel it."

She didn't reply. Let him guess what she thought for all she cared.

Her gaze wandered to the muscles of his back stretching the billowy white shirt. His tanned forearm flexed as he added another stick. He'd rolled up the legs of his loose white pants, revealing equally golden ankles and feet.

From his Richard Gere hair to his stern clean-shaven jaw, he was model material. His eyes, soft green like a mist-covered glade, penetrated straight to her soul. Ian posed a danger to her heart, no matter how he charged her body.

Remember what Grandma always said.

"Think with your logical brain, not with your romantic heart. Love does not put food in your mouth or a roof over your head."

Or decipher an ancient Welsh text.

"What can I do?" she asked as she stood, having nothing to do.

He rose from where he'd prepared the fire pit and walked to her, extending his hand. After a moment, she took it and stood beside him.

"Nothing. It's done. Are you ready?"

"For what?" Truly, the limits of reality had been shattered and anything seemed possible.

"For magick." He pulled her to the fire pit. Facing her, he tipped her chin up to gaze into his eyes. "What you see must remain secret. Do you agree?"

While still uncertain, she couldn't help being equally enchanted and curious. Being here, in this fairy-tale situation. "Yes."

His expression somber, he continued to stare for a minute more as if he were contemplating something. Then his mouth twitched on one corner. "We begin."

He shifted so they stood side by side, with her hand in his, facing the fire pit. He extended his free arm toward the sticks, his elegant fingers gracefully unfurling. A spark appeared at the base of the pyramid of driftwood and flames licked skyward.

He created fire! She carefully loosened the tight grip on Ian's hand and sucked in a breath. Her heart pounded in her chest. She slammed closed her open mouth.

He laughed and squeezed her hand, not letting her pull away. "You're not hurting me, Becca. And that is certainly the tamest reaction I've seen from a human."

He smiled down at her and all her practical lectures faded away with some of her tension.

Okay, so her sudden ESP made a little more sense. More questions than ever danced in her head. "So if I'm a human, what are you?"

"I'm not an alien, if that's what you're thinking. I'm a sorcerer."

She wrinkled her brow. "Like Merlin?"

For a brief moment, he frowned as if she'd said something wrong, something silly. "Yes, like Merlin. You see, Merlin is really a compilation of many myths from Wales, Ireland, and Scotland."

"Written by Geoffrey of Monmouth. Author of *Historia Regum Britanniae*. He popularized the King Arthur tales."

He stared at her. She'd surprised him, and that boosted her confidence. At least this knowledge provided a firmer foundation to stand on in this quicksand situation she'd stumbled into.

"You see, Ian, I am a librarian and a bibliophile. I majored in British literature, so I am quite familiar with Geoffrey's works."

"Ah." His Adam's apple bobbed as he seemed to assimilate this knowledge. This man disliked surprises as a control freak would. "I am of Myrddin's bloodline. *He* was the primary inspiration for Geoffrey's Merlin myths."

From the challenge she read in his eyes, he probably assumed she didn't believe him. She would surprise him again.

"Nice to meet you, Ian, descendant of Myrddin."

He barked out a full-throated laugh that reverberated straight down to their joined hands. "You are a strange woman, Becca."

She grinned. "Thank you. I think."

"Come on, let's get started. It'll be dark soon."

"What happens if we're still doing"—she paused, searching for the right word because she really did not know what he planned—"whatever and we can't find our way back."

He smiled and raised his hand to her cheek. "You'll be safe here."

His touch sent simultaneous chills and heat racing through her and she shivered. Words escaped her so she nodded and together they knelt on the blanket.

Facing her, he took a lock of her hair and rubbed it between his fingers. "I'm trying not to seduce you, Becca. I'm trying very hard." His husky voice shot a tremor through her, awakening a need she barely recognized.

She couldn't drag her gaze from his smoldering eyes as they reflected the fire's glow.

"Focus on why we're here." Were those her words?

His eyes narrowed for a second before cocking an eyebrow. "Place your right hand on my heart."

She had trouble following his directions with the blood thundering in her temples and her heart pounding in her chest. He helped her, moving aside the unbuttoned front so she touched his chest.

God, he makes me light-headed.

His skin blazed beneath her touch, and his heart thumped hard against her hand. He slid his right hand inside the open neckline of her gauzy shift to rest on her skin. Her breasts swelled in response to his touch.

Remember why we're here. Why are we here?

She desperately wanted his mouth on hers.

"Becca." His voice was gravelly. "I'm going to open now, drop my guard. You'll hear my thoughts, and I'll experience your emotions. Try to stay relaxed."

Relaxed? No fucking way. Her pulse raced, her heart pumped hard and fast, and she wanted to throw him on the ground and ride him. And he expected her to relax?

He gazed at her. Time stood still.

His body shook. How did she know he fought against letting go? She laid her free hand on his shoulder and he followed her lead, completing the circuit. An electric jolt ran up her arm where her hand lay over his heart, but she didn't pull away. Until now, she hadn't really known emotional intimacy.

"Breathe, Ian. I'm here. Breathe."

A great rush of air expelled from his lungs. His fingers tightened on her shoulder and tensed against her chest. Anxiety, greater than she'd ever experienced punched into her, churned in her stomach. She squeezed her eyes shut to help block out the intensity. Fear and rage followed, making her head pound and her hands clench into fists. Did he deal with this every day? How did he do it? How could he function?

"Becca. Becca, let it go. Let it wash through you, breathe it out."

Only his hand gripping her shoulder and anchoring her heart in her chest kept her aware enough to hear him, comprehend his words.

"Come on, darling."

She opened her eyes and focused on his concerned face. Using his eyes as her focal point, she breathed in unison with him. In, hold ten, then out. Over and over, she repeated the process until her heart rate slowed and her respiration leveled out.

His gaze dropped to her mouth and the wave of his desire crashed over her.

Chapter Four

*S*low *down, Branson. You just beat her up with your fear and fury. Give her a break.*

It was a mistake to bring her to this isolated spot. Magick without control could result in injury or unintended exposure to humans. How would it look for the chairman who oversaw the ethical use of magick to reveal the paranormal world? The seclusion worked against him now as his libido revved into overdrive.

She moistened her lips with her pretty pink tongue. She drew in a ragged breath. Her heart knocked against his palm. Her green eyes dropped to his mouth and he was lost.

"Becca."

She met his gaze and ran her hand from his shoulder to his cheek before leaning forward. Adrenaline shocked his system, increasing the urgency of his desire. He needed her. Now. No use denying his absolute hunger for her.

Her mouth brushed his. Her sweet, tentative

kiss tore at his control. To keep from scaring her with the raging passion he had no experience in leashing, he let her take the lead. He parted his lips, inviting her in. She nibbled at his mouth in gentle nips. Like fine Beaujolais, he savored the taste of her lips, the silky glide of them over his, keeping his response in tune with hers.

She ran her hand into his hair.

He trailed his fingers from her shoulder to the petal-smooth skin of her neck. She tilted her head, giving him access to more. Oh, yes, he wanted more. So much more.

She angled her mouth, mating it to his. He held his breath, the anticipation killing him. Her soft tongue dipped into his mouth, and he met it with calm deliberation, their tongues tangling in a slow first dance.

His control fraying, his heartbeat racing, he stroked her velvet cheek with his thumb. A whimper vibrated on his tongue. The last thread of control snapped. He fisted his hand in her hair at the nape of her neck, taking over the kiss. He devoured her, his tongue dominating hers, forceful, taking what he wanted.

His growled groan was answered by her softer moan. Her eyes, glazed with desire, stared into his.

"Ian, it's getting dark."

"You're right."

Making love with her here and now couldn't happen. He removed his hand from her dress. Cradling her face in his palms, he smiled. "Thank you. You freed me from my recent emotional hell."

Her brows drew together and her eyes narrowed. "Oh. Okay. You're welcome." She pulled her hands away and struggled to her feet. "Um, I guess we need to put out the fire."

What did he say? What did he do? He was an idiot. Again.

He stood and grabbed her by the shoulders to keep her still. "Are you okay?"

She didn't meet his gaze. Even though the sun slowly sank, taking with it the remaining light, her disappointment was clear in how her gaze remained cemented to the sand.

"Yes. I'm fine. I don't hear your thoughts or feel your emotions anymore."

So she didn't feel the connection anymore. Probably for the best, though the gnawing in his stomach and the tightness in his chest didn't match the sentiment.

He folded up the blanket and handed it to her. By lowering his hands, palms down, he extinguished the fire.

The sun, only a faint glow of orange on the edge of the sea, fled and turned the day into night. He took her hand and conjured a ball of light for a lantern to light the way. While her eyes widened, she said nothing. He needed to concentrate on the sounds of the forest as danger prowled after dark. A prayer offered to the gods couldn't hurt.

By the gods, let me return her safe and sound to the main house. I'll honor our agreement and help her with the scroll. She's already given me so much, my peace of mind, my control. A shame she pulled back on the beach. I would have given her pleasure beyond her wildest dreams. It's better this way. Better I didn't let her in completely. I already admire and desire her too much. If I touched her soul....

A branch cracked. Dry leaves crunched.

He opened to sense for nearby visitors...or predators.

Hunger. Lust. Not for sexual release but flesh and blood. Werewolf. He hoped it hunted alone.

He squeezed Becca's hand and received a return squeeze. With intense focus, he reached out to her, making a conscious connection.

Listen. Werewolf nearby. Adolescent and dangerous. He can't control his urges yet. I don't want to hurt him if I can help it. Do you understand?

Their eyes met over the light in his hand and she nodded, her mouth tight and eyes wide. Shock mixed with fear washed through him. He prayed she would trust the connection they had and not bolt.

Stay close. I can protect you if you do exactly as I say.

He closed his hand, extinguishing the light. Not a good idea to make it too easy for the wolf. Along the path he crept as quickly as he could, careful to avoid as many of the overhanging branches and roots underfoot as possible. When Becca tripped, he caught her.

He loved that she trusted him. He wouldn't trust someone else's decisions so quickly. He hadn't earned her trust. He wasn't worthy of her.

Leaves crunched. The wolf closed on them.

He picked up the pace, dragging her behind.

I have to get you to safety.

A stick broke a few feet away, sounding like a gunshot in the silent forest. The wolf launched itself, mouth agape, teeth bared to latch on and tear flesh. Ian held up his hands and the animal slammed into an invisible wall.

"I don't want to hurt you, boy," he warned the growling wolf. Through narrowed eyes, he murmured an ancient spell in Welsh. The wolf stopped growling, curled on the forest floor, and slept.

Come on, hurry. There may be more.

His heart drummed wildly in his chest. One of his own had stalked Becca, would have hurt her had she been alone.

He rushed into the Haus, Becca in tow, and bumped into Rekkus. Solid fellow that he was, Ian bounced off and stepped back. He drew Becca in close with an arm around her waist.

"Rekkus. There's a sleeping wolf about a half mile back on the trail from the private cove."

The head of security looked at Becca, raised his eyebrows then shook his head. "Your doing, I assume?"

Ian shrugged. "He wasn't very friendly."

Rekkus's brow furrowed. "Thank you. I'll take care of him." With a curt nod, he left.

Adrenaline from the encounter still zinging in his blood carried with it a euphoria at having beaten a foe, protected his woman. He'd missed the magical high. Between imprisonment in his office and locking down his powers, he'd lost a piece of his soul. Facing down a werewolf safely fed both his confidence and his libido. Did he dare shed his heavy mantle of responsibility to embrace his desires? Becca's ardor had cooled following the intense storm of their kiss.

One glance at Becca's face ignited a spark of hope. Her mouth quirked up and she shook her head in disbelief. "I feel like I just stepped out of a fairy tale."

With her hand small and warm in his hand, he had to agree. Happiness bloomed in his chest, replacing the knot caused by the loss of his wife. "Me, too." He couldn't help the goofy grin tugging at his lips.

"You were amazing." Her eyes sparkled as she stared up into his with a childlike wonder.

He picked a twig from her hair, a souvenir from their night hike, and handed it to her. "No, he's just a boy. I'm glad you're okay."

"I just don't know what to think. I'd always dreamed of waking up in a fairy tale and here I am."

"And you're handling it beautifully." They still stood in the lobby, Myron watching from her station. "Tired?"

She scoffed. "Are you kidding? No, couldn't sleep if I tried. I've got a few questions."

He silently thanked the gods for an opening. "We need some privacy."

Her eyebrow arched, stirring the embers of his passion. "Of course. Your room or mine?" Becca's sweet innocence fanned those embers to a sizzling flame. Heat suffused his belly, flowing like molten lava to every pore of his body. He wallowed in the intoxicating warmth and freed his tightly reined emotions. With one smooth movement, he scooped her up in his arms.

"Ian. Put me down." Despite her protests, her smile stretched across her face.

He elbowed the call button for the elevator and

closed his eyes in ecstasy when her lips grazed his jaw. Her silky mouth on his neck kicked up the blood pressure that had been dropping back to normal. Did she feel the blood pounding in his veins?

The elevator dinged and the doors slid open. Thank the gods the lift was empty because he wanted his mouth on hers. Now. He set her on her feet and framed her face with his hands. And lowered his mouth to hers.

He devoured her, his tongue pillaged, his teeth nipped at her bottom lip. He backed her against the wall and pressed his throbbing shaft to her belly.

Damn elevator. When the doors glided open, he dragged his mouth from hers and gulped in air. His body, tense with desire, ached for her. From the dazed look in her eyes, she wanted him just as much.

In a hurry to get to his room, he swept her off her feet and strode to the door. Too impatient to stop and unlock the door, he opened it with a flourish of his fingers. Magick helped open the door but wouldn't relieve the painful throbbing in his pants. Only Becca could remedy his ache.

He kicked the door closed and carried her to the bed. He took a moment to light a candle on the bedside table with the flick of his wrist before he covered her body with his. He couldn't get enough of her. Her delicious sweet lips eagerly responded to his demands. The wet heat of her mouth surrounded his tongue, and he couldn't help the obvious parallel to burying his cock inside her.

He had to touch her, skin to skin. He reached down and grabbed the hem of the loose cover-up.

With none of the subtlety he prided himself on, he tugged the garment off her, breaking his kiss for only a moment.

Finesse nonexistent now, she'd stripped him of his elegant veneer to his most primal form. He'd never felt so feral. He'd never felt so alive.

She worked at his shirt buttons but her fingers fumbled. His chest heaving, dragging in air, he stood. Her eyes widened but she didn't look away. She licked her kiss-reddened lips and sent a jolt through his system.

Quickly, he divested himself of shirt and pants. She raised her eyebrow at his lack of underwear. "Commando?"

"Comfortable." His voice sounded husky to his ears.

When her gaze raked his body, tremors raced through him as if she'd touched him. His engorged erection bobbed, drawing her attention. She licked her lips again and he wanted her mouth on him, tasting his essence. She'd done this to him, made him want her with an almost unbearable intensity. His fingers itched to slide up her legs to the juncture hidden by her conservative bathing suit bottom.

Her eyebrows drew together, and he wondered if she heard his thoughts. No sense in worrying now. Actions spoke louder than words.

He jerked his chin at her swimsuit. "Take it off."

Again, her brow furrowed and she frowned a bit. Maybe he'd have to do it for her. She surprised him by slowly removing the halter top and bottoms, her anxiety rolling off her. Shyness made her more desirable than all the sophisticated women he'd met on the East Coast.

She reclined, her weight resting on her bent arms, a slight bend at one knee. She shimmered perfect ivory against the sea blue of the comforter. While she was so gorgeous, so alluring, she was also completely uncomfortable naked. Soon she'd know how very lovely she was.

He lay next to her and rolled to his back. "Touch me."

Her little grin revealed a bit of confusion, but complete amused willingness. He couldn't take his eyes off her face as she leaned over to trace a finger over his bottom lip. He touched the tip of his tongue to her fingertip and she smiled.

She ran her fingers over his face, her gaze following their trail. He kept his gaze on her face, watched every expression flicker across her fine features. She enjoyed exploring him at her leisure. Being in control made her more comfortable. It made him crazy.

She followed the line of his jaw then traveled the length of his neck. No bone or muscle ignored. The contours of his collarbone, the bulge of his bicep—they all received her personal attention.

He closed his eyes to focus on controlling his reactions. Gentle circles drawn around his nipple jerked him to full attention. He opened his eyes to see her lean down and take his nipple between her lips.

"Becca." He clenched his fists to keep from grabbing her, rolling her over, and driving into her.

"You like this?" Her amused voice taunted him. She liked torturing him, the vixen.

"Too much." He drew in a ragged breath when

she sucked his nipple in her hot mouth then rolled it between her teeth.

"Do you want me to stop?"

Never. He could stand a little more torture. Maybe. "No."

His eyes closed, he tried to relax but every touch, every lick burned like a live wire. Delicious torture.

Her hands stroked in tandem down his sides to his hips, stopping to run her thumbs along his hipbones. His belly jerked at her open-mouthed kiss on his skin. She swirled her tongue around his navel then delved into the depression. Nerve endings throughout his pelvis exploded with pleasure and anticipation. Her tongue distracted him from her hand until it closed around the swollen shaft.

His hips thrust off the bed. A gasp exploded from his lips. "Becca," he warned.

"Just give me a minute, Ian. Please."

He opened his eyes again. Her red hair flaming in the candlelight, she moved forward and pressed her lips softly to the tip of his cock. Entranced, he watched her sip the drop from the tip then circle the head with her tongue. Blood surged, further engorging his throbbing member. If she took him into her mouth, he'd come instantly. He didn't want that. Yet.

"Minute's up," he said, grinding the words out through clenched teeth.

With a sudden move, he flipped her on her back. He wouldn't be so gentle. He needed his mouth on her. Everywhere. Now.

Her scent of lavender and sea spray surrounded him. Her pink nipples beckoned his kiss and he devoured them, taking first one then the other into his mouth. He sucked, grazed with his teeth, and licked them while his hands ran over her silky skin. Her ragged gasps ratcheted up his urgency. He moved his hand over her quivering belly then cupped her mound. His mouth followed with rough kisses. He slid down the bed and parted her legs, kneeling between them. Blood pounded in his temples, lust raged in his gut. Nothing existed but her.

She was his.

Her eyes widened as he reached beneath her hips and jerked them up. Impatient, needy, he bent his head and took a long lick. Her moan spurred another lick and another. He sucked her greedily as she thrashed against his hold.

"Ian."

"Becca, you taste so good." He flicked her clit and she arched further off the bed. Oh, how he wanted her to come in his mouth.

"Stop." She panted and trembled. "I want to come with you. Inside me."

If he didn't enter her right now, he'd come outside her, all over her. Not the way he wanted. This time.

From the drawer, he retrieved a packet, ripped it open, and rolled on the condom in record time. Just the touch of his own hand had his cock throbbing painfully.

He stretched out on top of her and kissed her gently. She sucked his tongue, sending a white-hot shock to his loins.

All restraint vanished.

Urgency reigned as he hooked a hand under

one knee, his mouth still on hers while he glided his body back and forth over hers. Her nipples grazed his chest, her skin like satin against his stomach. Each time his staff nudged her slick opening, he slid back. Each time he touched her most private part, she whimpered.

He wanted to hear her scream his name.

Surging forward, he entered her in one fluid thrust, her scream echoing in his head. She moaned and restlessly moved beneath him. Her fingers dug into his shoulders, the pain a heady drug.

"Are you all right?" He had to make himself ask because every part of him wanted to drive into her over and over. But he'd poured all his fear and rage into her earlier. She'd fearlessly taken it with compassion. He only wanted passion and pleasure for her now.

She opened her glazed eyes and glared at him. "If you dare stop now, I'll kill you."

He laughed aloud. This woman surprised him, amused him, and inspired a wild lust. "Fair enough. I have to warn you, I have a lot of pent-up passion."

"Yeah, it's been a long time for me, too. I don't want slow and sweet."

He shook his head and smiled at her. "By the gods, woman, neither do I."

He raised her hands over her head, lacing them with his own. Sliding out, he paused. Her hips rose off the bed to drive him back in. He thrust again and again, her hips driving him deeper. Sweat dripped down his back. He burned inside and out. Her muscles gripped him ever tighter while her high-pitched moans turned low and guttural.

Hotter, deeper, harder, more.

He released her hands to slide his hands under her back to anchor her in place. So close to a cataclysmic climax.

"Ian."

Her body jerked as every muscle in her body clenched. Colors exploded behind his closed eyelids, and the roaring rose to a crashing crescendo in his head. His body, coiled in unbearable tension, released in ecstasy.

Her inner muscles spasmed, pleasure flooding into him as his passion poured out. Only peace remained but for how long? Had this been a mistake?

Chapter Five

I *must be crazy.*
How could she feel so safe in the midst of such lunacy?

Becca stretched within the confines of Ian's embrace. His arm held her close, and his coarse chest hair tickled her back as he molded his body to hers. Warm, even breaths stirred her hair over her ear while his heart thudded slowly and rhythmically against her back.

Ian's erection, hard and hot, pressed to her backside seemed real enough.

He was a sorcerer. Werewolves were real. Ian could start fire with a flick of his wrist, stop a werewolf in his tracks, and cast a sleeping spell. What kind of place was Wiccan Haus? True, she'd come hoping for some psychic insight. Was it such a stretch sorcerers exist? Fairy tales weren't real but she knew what she'd seen, what she'd felt.

The revelation of the existence of magickal beings didn't scare her as much as her intense attraction and absolute connection with Ian. How could she not have a deep connection when she'd been in his head and heart? No way to deny he touched her more deeply than any other man.

Falling in love would be useless. With only five more days together, they'd both have to return to the real world. Well, at least for her; the magick would continue for him. She sighed to relieve the heaviness in her chest. Until then, if he still wanted her, she'd enjoy the magick they kindled.

As if he read her thoughts, he snuggled closer and stroked his shaft against her butt. "You're thinking so hard, you woke me up."

She drew a moan from him with a wiggle of her hips. "You know you don't owe me for helping you."

He froze. "You think we made love because I'm grateful?"

While she couldn't see him, she could not mistake the hurt in his words.

"Well...."

He cupped her breast and ran his thumb over her nipple. She sucked in a breath from the shock of need that shot through her. He flexed his hips, sliding his erection into the gap between her thighs. Wetness flowed from her well-used body.

With his lips nuzzled against her neck, alternatively licking and kissing, he said, "I'll admit the first time may have had a tiny bit to do with gratitude. But the second, third, and fourth times were absolutely for pleasure. Completely because I want you more than I've ever wanted any woman."

His hand kneaded her breast and she bit back a moan but it came out as a whimper. Pleasure? She'd never experienced such intense pleasure.

"Wait. We didn't have sex four times." Her

body responded to his like they'd always been lovers. Her hips matched his rhythm, and she arched her head back to expose more of her neck to his plundering mouth.

"One, we didn't have sex. We made love." He moved his hand from her breast to her thigh and hooked his elbow under her knee, opening her up. "Two, this is round four." He shifted and thrust into her in one smooth action.

"Oh, God, Ian."

He filled her so perfectly, she couldn't form a single coherent thought. Her mind clouded, all sounds faded to background noise for the drumming of her heart. She willingly submitted to his spell. His motion ebbed and flowed much more smoothly this morning. He was calmer, more relaxed. Last night, she'd fed his passion; this morning, he fed her soul.

She didn't care, she wanted him. Only him.

More, deeper, she undulated her body to please him. Her heart pumped harder every time he moaned.

He lowered her leg, his hot steely shaft still sheathed inside her body. She waited. He'd taught her positions from the Kama Sutra last night. Turned out he was a yoga master. Which one would he employ for her pleasure this morning?

"Slowly, move onto all fours then lower your chest to the bed."

Ah, some variation of doggie style.

"This is called the elephant."

When she complied, her cheek pressed to the sheet, he leaned forward, his chest to her back, his mouth on her shoulder.

"With you, it's more like the goddess."

She felt like a goddess with him. With him, she forgot her inhibitions.

His arms hooked under hers and grasped her shoulders. He surrounded her. There was nowhere he didn't touch her. He filled her, wrapped around her. Where did she end and he begin? Like yin and yang, they entwined, two parts of one whole.

For what seemed like hours, he held her close, the embrace sacred, intimate, loving.

Someone had once said reality was overrated. In this case, she agreed. If this week turned out to be a dream, she didn't want to wake up.

With a tiny flex of his hips, he snapped her out of her reverie. Instantly, she lived in the moment and nothing mattered but the slide of his body on hers.

He held her tightly, rotating his hips so his thrusts were short and shallow. Last night, he'd overwhelmed her with a full-on attack. His hands and mouth ignited a wildfire that burned hot and out of control. This morning, he initiated a surgical strike—a deliberate spark and controlled rate of consumption. He would consume her, of that she was sure. As sure she would savor every sensation.

"Becca, you are so damn incredible."

He set another spark with his open-mouthed kisses on the back of her neck. Electric shock zapped her inner muscles. They clenched and her hips jerked. His teeth sank into her skin, incurring another involuntary reaction. His hips jolted hard into her and she gasped. "By the gods, Becca, you make me wild."

Her breath rasping as she dragged it in and

panted it out, she uttered one word. "Good."

His control snapped with a gasp. Strong fingers dug into her shoulders; his hips drove forward in one hard thrust.

"I wanted, I needed this time to be for you." His voice low and husky, he grunted the words and punctuated each with a feral thrust.

If he said anything else, it was lost on her as her world collapsed to the hurricane roaring in her ears. His body crashed into hers, wave after intense wave. She panted with each impact. He tightened his embrace, his compromise to releasing his wild lust.

Every muscle tensed, every glide of his hair and skin on her sending jolts of pleasure. Her muscles coiled tighter and harder. So much tension, she couldn't stand more.

The pressure built, compressed until she imploded with a scream ripped from her soul. Her body froze in place while muscles spasmed. Her skin tingled all over. One mighty thrust, one echoing yell, and he fell forward on her.

"Becca, darling, are you all right?"

No man had given her such ecstasy. No man ever treated her with such care. She gave in to her overflowing heart and fell flat in love.

Swallowing her sorrow for the new ill-fated love she'd found and would ultimately lose, she lied.

"I'm fine." She would use the days to discover what she could from the scroll and spend the nights in the arms of the only man who would ever fill her romantic heart.

***

"You're amazing."

Becca marveled at the ease with which Ian translated the scroll. Written in ancient Welsh, only a few scholars in the world had the knowledge necessary to read it. Fate had smiled on her when she met him.

She still wondered at his claim of ownership, and she would get to the bottom of his assertion after she'd gotten her answers. Better to move toward her goal than argue about ownership of a scroll. Her dream of finding out her father's identity took precedence. He might still be alive. She might have more family. Even one distant cousin would be better than being alone.

Her mission seemed simple, but the man next to her filled her heart and set her free. During breakfast, at a secluded table in the corner, he'd opened his world to her, quietly pointing out the paranormal guests. She'd nodded, enthralled by the knowledge that so many extraordinary people lived secretly among humans. Unwilling to disturb the status quo, she asked no questions. If she did, he might lock away the part he'd shared so openly.

"Look here," he said, pointing to a part of the text near the top of the parchment. "A spell for ridding a man of lice. I needed this a couple of years ago when Allan got a nasty case of the buggers."

"Allan?"

With a smile, he turned to look at her. "My six-year-old. He's what keeps me going."

"Oh." A son? Was there a Mrs. Sorcerer back home?

"Yes, he's finally coming out of his shell. He's bonded with Cassidy, sees her as a mother figure."

"Mmm hmm." Who was Cassidy? Housekeeper? Nanny? Or girlfriend?

"Sweetheart, Cassidy is Allan's teacher. And I'm a widower."

After a moment, when he didn't supply any more information, she sighed. She'd never get the chance to meet his little boy, see them together. Swallowing the lump in her throat, she refocused on the scroll. Somewhere in this document clues to her own family lay hidden. Remaining true to her goal took precedence. Right?

"These spells don't help me, Ian."

He sat back and chuckled. "I know, darling. I know. It's just this is an ancient spell book. It's exciting to me." He patted her hand. "You can go take a nap, if you want. I'll work on this and let you know if there's anything relevant."

Something in his voice wasn't right. Why was he trying to get rid of her?

"No. In fact, it might save time for you to translate it aloud and I'll write it down. That way I can refer to it later."

His brows drew together. He didn't want her to know everything in the text. Why?

"Sure. Sounds like a great idea. Do you have a notebook?"

Her stomach twisted because he was holding something back from her. "I'll just go get it. Be right back."

She gave him a tight smile and ground her teeth on the way to the door.

The door opened, startling her for the second day in the exact same way, though with a different man. Cyrus Rowan entered and nodded cordially to her.

"Good morning, Becca." His gaze swept to Ian. Silent communication occurred. Most people would have missed it, but she'd made people-watching her hobby. She had to hurry.

Why did everyone seem to know more than she did?

"Chairman."

Ian ignored the spark of irritation when Cyrus addressed him with his title. He wouldn't have come without a purpose.

"Cyrus. How are you?"

The dark brother shrugged. "As long as I stay out of Sarka's way, I'll be fine. She's still pissed about the werewolf attacking you and Ms. Jones. She raked Rekkus over the coals."

"Good thing he's got a thick skin. How is the pup?"

"Had to deal with Rekkus so he's a little cowed at the moment." Cyrus glanced at the parchment held open with a couple of crystal paperweights. "This yours?"

"No," he said unnecessarily. Cyrus knew the scroll belonged to Becca.

"I had a conversation with your friend. You may want to know—"

Ian raised his hand to stop Cyrus. "Don't worry, Cyrus. I have everything under control."

Cyrus's dark eyebrow cocked as he narrowed his eyes. "You're sure?"

"Positive."

"As you wish."

The big man rolled his eyes and muttered as he

stalked to the door. He passed Becca in the doorway as she hurried in with her notebook and pen. Ian's heart jerked and jealousy clawed in his belly when Cyrus gave his woman an overly thorough appraisal.

His woman.

Damn it. Whether he liked it or not, the fates had chosen this woman as his mate. He didn't want another mate, didn't want the pain of losing another part of his heart. Any proclaimed mate of the council was a prime target.

He smiled at her as she approached. Thankfully, his balance had returned following the ritual on the beach. Calmer, he could shield his thoughts and emotions though sharing his entire being with her called to his heart. Only his chosen mate could fulfill all his needs, make him whole. Duty and honor refused to put her in harm's way.

Her irritation showed in the jut of her chin and the tightness of her jaw. No reason to hold anything back from the translation. No reason to hold anything back from her at all. After the spell, she'd forget everything. Even him.

He shoved down the bitterness rising in his throat. Letting her go would be a knife to his heart, but she'd never be safe with him. Given the choice, she would take the leap of faith and go with him. She trusted him; she'd shown her absolute faith last night when the werewolf attacked. He refused to lose another person. Allan's foiled abduction proved how desperate the rebel factions were. He shuddered to think what they'd do to sweet Becca.

Now seated next to him, she watched him with a furrowed brow. Had she asked him a question?

He focused on the scroll. "How did this come

into your possession?"

She leaned back in the chair. "When my grandmother died, this was in her safe deposit box." She raised her right hand and twisted the ring on her finger. "This, too."

He took her hand in his to better see the ring. A cabochon ruby winked in an antique copper scrolled setting, the kind he'd seen on members of his own family. The ring spun freely on her middle finger, indicating it had been made for a man's hand.

"How did they come to your grandmother?"

"I believe they belonged to my father."

"What was your father's name?" Maybe the man had been a thief or con man, not that he'd tell her that.

"I don't know." Her quiet answer expressed more confusion and disappointment than the actual words. Pieces fell into place. Not all of them, but enough to explain her lack of self-confidence.

"Your mother's and grandmother's last name is Jones?"

"Yes. Was."

She impressed him as she battled back tears. "I'm sorry."

"I don't remember my mother. She died when I was only three. It's strange, though. I feel like she's near me."

"She is, Becca. Our loved ones watch over us."

A soul-deep sigh escaped her. "I just want to know who my father is. Maybe he's alive. Maybe he doesn't know I exist."

She was lost and needed to find her home. His heart broke a little.

Perhaps the scroll could provide clues, but

would her father be an honorable man? Or a para who might hurt her? Or worse, be a member of the Mundus Novus or another faction? This scroll had been lost for centuries; one of her ancestors could have been a witch or a sorcerer who'd forsaken their oath to do no harm. *Power corrupts.*

Only one task remained: translate the scroll.

Two hours later, Ian had gained insight into his forefather but hadn't found anything to help Becca with her quest. Her drumming fingers and frequent sighs didn't diminish his delight in his ancestor's words.

"Healing potions and scrying spells. This is no more helpful than a cookbook."

Becca banged the pen down on the open notebook and rested her forehead on the table. After a couple of breaths, she sat up with a jerk and a frown. "I'm sorry, Ian. That must sound really disrespectful to you. Sacrilegious. I don't mean any harm."

I don't mean any harm. If she had a paranormal ancestor, at least she already had the right mind-set.

A shiver ran up his spine. Fearful certainty that she'd be in peril as his mate lodged firmly in his throat. Her safety was his paramount concern. Sharp pain seared his heart. In three short days, she'd branded her name on his soul. No way he could deny her as his mate. She fit him body, heart, and soul. Letting her go would cut him off at the knees. Seeing her hurt would kill him.

No perfect answer came to him. He would handle it the best he could.

"Sweetheart, I know you were hoping for a clue.

Maybe there's one deeper in the scroll." He rubbed her shoulder. "We've been at this for a while. Let's take a break. Take a walk. You'll feel better."

Walking away from the scroll was hard. These writings sprang from Myrddin's head, flowed from his fingers, uttered from his very lips. He'd have all the time in the world to translate the incantations after he returned home. Once Becca returned to her home, safe and sound, he'd grieve the loss of his heart and soul over the ancient document.

Until the time to let her go, he would make memories to tuck away. Later, alone in the wee hours of the night, he'd take them out and hold them tight and try to remember why he'd let his soul mate go.

Chapter Six

*H**ow can there be so many psychics and so few answers?*

"Ian, we didn't find anything," Becca said as he led her to a quiet table in the dining room.

People stared at them. Ian clearly hadn't told her everything. More than once staff members had almost called him something that started with "ch." It didn't matter if he were a prince or a pauper. Every minute of their time together would be treasured. She pushed aside the nagging voice insinuating he should trust her implicitly with every secret. It wasn't as if they were planning a lifetime together.

He pulled out her chair, ever the consummate gentleman, ever controlled. After she eased into her seat and he'd relaxed into his own, she released a heavy sigh.

She'd hoped to find at least a sign to her path, some crumb to follow to her father's history.

Tears threatened. Time was running out. Three

days of translating the scroll yielded no clues to her parentage. Ian tried to hide his excitement, but she could see how much the scroll meant to him. When she left the island, she would give it to him. He loved the old moldering parchment text; to her, it represented a means to an end.

She gritted her teeth because she used Ian, too. He translated the text so she could find a clue to her father's identity. Even though she loved him, she used him for his knowledge and skill. While the scroll intrigued him, she had no doubt he helped her because he liked her, lusted for her. He never mentioned the other "l" word. Undeniably, their relationship was temporary.

She would take him with her in her heart.

His son needed him. He'd told her about how Allan shut down after losing his mother. Ian had not spoken of his own grief about her death, but she'd sensed his guilt. Something about his job had put her in jeopardy, and Allan had witnessed his mother's death.

She wanted to take Ian in her arms to comfort him. She wished to meet Allan and get to know him, but he had his path and she had hers. Her heart ached at the thought of going home without him. She would go on. Finding the truth about her father might soothe the pain.

"Becca, I can help you. My way."

She smiled. "That's okay, Ian. I don't want to impose on you anymore than I already have."

A muscled jumped in his jaw. "You're not imposing. You haven't asked me to do anything I didn't want to do." He pulled her into his arms.

Leaning into his warm embrace, she inhaled his

now familiar scent. For the first time in her life, she felt whole. "What can you do?"

His smile held a secret. "Much more than you can imagine."

She grinned and chuckled. "More than control fire?"

He raised a cocky eyebrow. "Much more."

What the hell. She didn't have anything to lose.

She had been curious about his abilities. She'd reined in her vivid imagination, but now she wondered. Could he fly? Make things disappear?

Over a quiet meal, she sensed his forced enthusiasm as he distracted her with immaterial small talk about the weather, movies, and music. Who cared what temperature it was in New York City in the summer? Screw the weather. Screw everything.

Doubts she'd be able to walk away from him built like a thunderhead on a humid summer day. Who was she fooling? She'd leave with her heart broken. Worse, would she even have a shred of evidence to follow to find her father's identity? Would she care?

Her hand clenched into a fist. Bitterness rose in her throat, burning, stinging. She squeezed her eyes shut and tried to force her stomach to stop churning.

His warm hand covered hers.

"Shh. Becca, it'll be all right. I'll make it all right. I swear."

Her frustration and anxiety melted away with the certainty he'd keep his word. Hope sprouted.

***

"Isn't it dangerous, Ian? Remember the last time?"

Apprehension skittered up her spine as Becca trekked through the woods back to the secluded beach. An owl hooted and she started, surprised.

Ian's fingers squeezed her hand. "Darling, you are safe with me. Besides, Rekkus dressed those young wolves down. I guarantee they are locked down at the bunker, battling each other on some video game."

"Okay." Still, something was off. Something wasn't right.

"Come on. What you'll see will amaze you."

"You amaze me."

"You humble me, Becca."

He shifted the bag he'd stuffed with a blanket and candles as they arrived at the cove. After assisting her down to the beach, he dropped the bag and pulled her to him. Sinking into his kiss, she struggled with the rising disappointment roiling in her stomach.

Tears welled in her eyes. He wiped the moisture from her cheeks. His voice low and rough, he said, "You do not know how much this hurts me, too. I've never felt like this with anyone."

"What about your wife?"

A sad smile turned up the corners of his lips. "I loved her. Of course, I did. But she was my friend. We got along. Really, more a contract than a relationship." His lips caressed her forehead, the tip of her nose, her cheeks. "This, us, is completely different. I can't control what I feel for you. You make me feel so much it almost hurts."

"Me, too."

He stared into her eyes for what seemed like minutes before he sucked in a breath. "Let's find out what this scroll knows."

He spread the blanket on the sand. Candles circled the blanket. With a flick of Ian's wrist, the flames speared up on their wicks.

With the full moon glinting off the calm waters of the sea, this place, this man entranced her.

They knelt on the blanket, their knees touching. He gazed into her eyes and placed the scroll between them. Chanting in a foreign tongue—probably Welsh—Ian laid his hands on the ancient parchment.

What he said was anyone's guess.

Wind swirled about them with the unfamiliar chant, yet the candles continued to flicker. Like a benign tornado, air spun visibly around them, separating them from anything and everything else. The moon, ripe and bright, shone down on them like a spotlight as if all the magic in the world centered on them. Who knew? Truth was stranger than fiction.

Ian's eyes glittered, lit from within. Green fire danced in their depths.

God help me. I'm getting giddy and silly.

A smile stretched across his face, revealing his perfect teeth. "I'd forgotten the simple joy of magick. I got so bogged down in the day-to-day business of governing, I lost the connection." He looked at his hands in wonder as if he didn't recognize them then chuckled and clasped them together like caging a firefly gently between his palms. With a single motion, he threw his hands to the sky, releasing a shower of periwinkle sparks into the swirling winds.

She gaped at the spectacle then lowered her gaze to the happy man before her. Wide smile, relaxed features, intense eyes, he let his guard completely down and let her in. His pleasure warmed her heart. His smile faded and he firmed his mouth.

"Let's find out about this scroll."

Ah, back to business. With a nod as the only acknowledgment, Becca fought the sinking of her heart. He was not hers to lose. Their relationship could only be temporary. How would she ever forget a man like Ian?

With one hand cradling the scroll, he took her hands and placed them on the parchment. Laying his other hand on top, he began chanting. Her rational mind identified the words as foreign while her intuitive side, the side that had never questioned magick, understood every one.

"Myrddin, father of my father, the first and the evermore, grant our wish to see the past. We wish to understand the significance of the product of your mind and your soul. We do not seek glory or power or riches, only answers. Let it be."

Murmuring began, like a rustling of leaves, building to a roar. The vortex of wind changed to fire. A scream stuck in her throat.

Let it wash over you. Through you. Don't fight it, love. Breathe.

His familiar, beloved voice in her mind calmed her. If he said it would be all right, it would be.

The flames lowered, the noise dulled, and the winds died. Before them, a watery pale blue wall shimmered with images of a young couple leaving a cave.

Myrddin.

Who was the woman?

He paused for a moment then gripped her hand. Had he connected with his ancestor in some metaphysical way? Like revisiting a past life? How did the scroll play a role in her own past?

Ian interrupted her curiosity.

Her name is Anwyn. I've never heard Myrddin had a lover at this time of his life. Nor the name Anwyn. Only of his sister bringing him food and supplies from time to time.

Anwyn, whose long red hair riotously curled about her face, clung to Myrddin. His eyes squeezed closed as he pulled her into a tight embrace. No sound resonated from the wavering scene, but the utter anguish was palpable. Myrddin raised his head, murmured to Anwyn, and unwound her arms from him. Clearly, he was sending her away, and it killed them both inside.

Becca's heart clenched as a fist of misery tightened in her chest. Her heartache mirrored Anwyn's. She would leave her love in a couple of days. How would she learn to live without the man who made her hopes and dreams reality? He was her heart.

As Anwyn shambled away, her sight obviously obscured by tears, Myrddin hung his head and tore at his hair. He dropped to his knees and rocked forward, planting his forehead on the bare ground.

The scene dispersed like mist in the late morning sun.

Ian turned her face toward him with his fingers

on her chin. "Darling, don't cry."

"I can't help it." She accepted the handkerchief he offered and blew her nose. "Did you find out how the scroll relates to me?" With luck, he'd communicated with Myrddin on a psychic level to get the answers she needed.

"Yes. Your ancestor Anwyn carried his baby. We're very distantly related cousins. Probably at least thirty times removed."

Having a common ancestor from centuries before didn't faze her. What rocked her was how fate seemed to weigh more than free will. And that neither of them seemed willing to fight for love.

"I guess that makes us kissing cousins." She tried for a laugh but instead a sob broke from her lips. Sorrow swamped her. "She left him, just like I'll leave you. Both our hearts broken."

He shimmered before her watery eyes. "Be mine then, *fy nghariad.*"

Sure she hadn't heard correctly, she shook her head. "Be yours?"

His crooked smile didn't quite meet his eyes. "Yes. Mate your soul with mine."

Her world crumbling, her heart breaking, she wordlessly agreed. Why not? The memory of one perfect night with her white knight to embrace when she returned to the real world.

"How?" She sniffed and wiped her face on her arms.

"Listen to your heart and your soul. Magick is in your blood. If you let go, we will unite."

She nodded, her heart blocking any words from escaping her lips.

He cradled her face in his hands like she was

the most precious work of art or delicate artifact. "We kiss. See us together in your mind; let your soul come to mine." He nipped at her lips. "You'll lose your breath, but I won't let anything bad happen to you. Trust me."

"I do, Ian. I love you."

He smiled, this time with his eyes. "I love you, too, Becca. Always."

He kissed her gently, brushing her mouth lightly, teasing her lips apart with a swipe of his tongue. With a whimper, she opened to him, sliding her tongue along his in an intimate dance.

She allowed her mind to drift. Fog and mist swirled around his body in the distance. They floated closer, feet never touching the ground.

Their bodies twined; their mouths met; their souls fused. Bright light burst, blinding her and heating her body. Lightheaded blackness began to suck her under as her lungs began to burn.

His voice whispered in her head, a port in the storm. *Trust me.*

I do. Always.

***

"What the fuck did you do, Chairman?"

Cyrus stalked toward him, fury turning his normally stoic face into a mask of rage. Rage pulsed off him, bouncing off Ian in waves. His emotional barrier crumbled. Aware they were in the lobby, Ian checked to see who else was around. Thank the gods only Myron stood guard at her desk, flipping her ever-present cards.

Ian didn't need this shit this morning. He

pulled himself together as best he could. Sleepless hours grieving had robbed him of the peace he'd found since arriving at Wiccan Haus, since finding Becca Jones.

He faced Cyrus who stood with a stiff, someone-pissed-in-his-oatmeal stance.

"What did you do to Becca, Branson?"

Fear gripped his heart. "What do you mean? Is she hurt?"

Cyrus's nostrils flared.

"No, she's just lost." He poked a finger in Ian's chest. "What did you do? What the fuck kind of magick did you do to her?" His gaze dropped to Ian's hand where a ruby ring glinted on his pinky. "Did you wipe her memory so you could steal that scroll and her ring?" Cyrus grabbed Ian's shirt and twisted. "You bastard. You sicken me." With an impatient shove, he thrust Ian away from him like a steaming, stinking bag of dog shit.

"What's wrong with her?" *Oh, fuck. What have I done?*

"Like you care, you asshat." With a glance at Ian's face, he clenched his jaw, seeming to reassess the situation slightly. "She's walking around in a daze, and she doesn't remember you at all. As if part of her mind is gone."

Ian scrubbed his hands over his scruffy face. He knew better. Of course, he knew better. Wiccan code warned every spell must be done with the right intention. Whatever energy sent out inevitably came back threefold.

After mating their souls—and allowing himself a few treasured moments of true peace and tranquility—he'd cast a spell to wipe any memory of him from her brain. He'd spared her the pain of losing their love.

He'd cast the spell also to protect her from her heritage. She'd descended from Myrddin the sorcerer, and magick ran in her blood. If she never knew, she'd never develop those powers and never be in danger.

Ian had to see her to know what side effects the spell had created. Cyrus stood in his way.

"Where is she?" Ian had to determine if she was fine.

"Why? You already know all there is to know, don't you?"

"Do you?"

"Yes, and I tried to warn you, Chairman." Cyrus sneered the title, his lip curling in disgust. "She's an innocent, but she deserves to know who she is, what she is. You left her defenseless. Sooner or later, her abilities will present, and she'll question her sanity. Or she'll discover her ancestry another way and everything may come back to her." The big man's eyes narrowed. "What will you do then, Chairman?"

Helplessness, double what he'd arrived with, hammered him, along with a strong sucker punch of fury to the chest.

Fuck, what the hell does Cyrus expect from me? What do any of them expect? I don't need this shit. Why the hell do I have to shoulder all the responsibility?

Anger coiled in his belly and the muscles in his biceps tensed. He shoved Cyrus back. Hard. Cyrus stumbled a couple of steps before planting his feet and clenching his fists. Ian ground his teeth and balled his own fists, ready to take on the dangerous

Rowan brother. Heedless that Cyrus would surely beat him to a bloody pulp, Ian could not control his baser emotions.

Trixie's voice caught his attention. "This way, Becca. We'll have some breakfast." She spoke as if to a child.

Ian turned his head, dread sliding into his heart, displacing the furious tension.

Becca.

Trixie, ever serene, guided Becca with her arm hooked through hers. Confusion and frustration rammed into his gut. Ian could not shut out the emotions slamming into him, especially not his mate's. His own sorrow and loss almost brought him to his knees.

He turned back to Cyrus to apologize.

Thunk.

Sharp pain erupted from his jaw. He wiggled it, wincing from the sting to test it. It wasn't broken. Cyrus's anger sapped slightly; he absently rubbed his knuckles.

Ian sighed. He had no desire to fight back. He deserved a beating for hurting Becca with a thoughtless, selfish spell. Ultimately, he'd erased her memory to avoid his own guilt. He'd gladly have taken the backlash. Instead, sweet Becca suffered.

Worse, he couldn't take it back, couldn't undo what he'd done.

***

Having everyone's emotions bombard him drove Ian mad. To get away, he ran the trails on the island. Lungs burning, muscles like jelly, he pushed until he reached exhaustion. Breathless and depressed, he stumbled over a root near where the wolf had attacked them.

If only he'd trusted his powers to protect her. If only he'd fully taken her as his mate, taken her into his world, into his life.

He lay on his back and stared up into the overhanging branches. Had sorrow so besieged Myrddin after sending his woman and their baby away that he'd gone crazy? The historical record supported the crazed wild man in the Welsh woods legend. He'd gone on to become a powerful sorcerer. Would he have been so powerful with a mate?

"Ian?"

Again, Trixie appeared. He'd understood her to be one of the human Wiccan Haus staff. Maybe he was confused. Anything seemed possible at this point.

She stood over him for a moment, seeming to ponder his prone position on the ground. She dropped to the ground and folded her legs in her familiar pose. With a tilt to her head, she gazed at him.

"Ian. You are troubled."

Her serenity grated on his frayed nerves. At least *her* emotions weren't beating him up.

He huffed out a breath. 'Thought Cemil was the empath."

Her eyebrow raised and one corner of her mouth quirked, acknowledging his sarcasm. "I don't have to be psychic to recognize pain."

No, his pain probably radiated from him like a reactor in terminal meltdown. Anyone not deaf, dumb, and blind could see how fucked up he was.

"How is Becca?"

"Lost. Strange how she doesn't know who you are."

Pain seared through his veins, but he clamped his lips shut. Trixie seemed a lot smarter than anyone gave her credit for. Smart people kept their mouths closed and their ears open.

"You've broken her, Ian."

"I—"

"No, just listen. She's lost her sense of who she is. And I suspect you're feeling a bit the same. You think you're protecting her, but by taking away her knowledge of the scroll and the ring, you stole a part of her."

Trixie easily rose to her feet and pinned him with a pitying look. "The thing is, you need her."

He shook his head. His inner voice—or maybe Myrddin—called him a liar.

She frowned at him. "You need her to ground you. As an empath, emotions are electrical impulses that can overload your system. Strong feelings are like lightning, but when you are grounded, you can channel the power into the earth safely."

He could not deny the truth of her statement. He'd hoped the experience of being with Becca would carry him through the worst onslaughts of fury, passion, and anxiety. In fact, sending her away decreased his ability to control his reactions tenfold.

"You need her as your mate, too. You're meant for each other. I see it. I feel it. Make it right."

"I can't." He hated the helplessness smothering him. *Fuck.*

"Sarka can." Trixie shrugged. Nobody liked

asking Sarka Rowan for help. With her razor-sharp tongue and acidic attitude, nobody liked asking her anything.

As Trixie ran off down the trail back to the Haus, he considered her observations. She'd nailed him on every point. The answer was simple yet hard to swallow. Prostrating himself before Sarka, the Dark One, tore at his pride, yet he must.

He dragged himself to his feet and shuffled along the trail in Trixie's wake.

A stiff drink—or three—would give him liquid courage before facing the dark sorceress in her lair.

May the gods take pity on me.

Chapter Seven

*H*ere we go.
　　"So you made a huge fecking mess, did you, Chairman?"

Ian detested needing help. He especially hated to petition Sarka Rowan for it. The staff called her the Dark Sister or simply the Dark One not only for her black hair and olive skin. Her soul and personality exuded an ominous edge, like a rabid wolf hiding in a cave ready to attack. Though the Syndicate members appreciated Cyrus's service and sacrifice, none truly trusted Sarka. Her mighty powers raised concerns within the ruling body, as she refused to socialize with or participate in any committees. Naturally, the Syndicate feared the unknown.

He swallowed against a tiny frisson of uneasiness threatening to lodge in his throat.

Clothed in a black dress that emphasized her long, lean body, she stood from her chair and one of her eyebrows winged up. With one hand on her hip and the haughty raise of her chin, she personified the strength and grace of a prima ballerina about to take the stage as the black swan. And the danger of a coiled, hissing cobra.

Frustration and desperation roiling inside his stomach, he dug his nails into the palm of one hand and pushed the door shut with the other. His control frayed with each passing second.

"I need your help." His voice trembled. She'd heard it; her smirk confirmed it. Her glee at his situation irritated him, infuriated him.

"What is the problem?"

There she stood, so smug in her safe little world.

He reined back his anger. She had not caused his problem. He hadn't caused it either.

"I need to regain my center, my focus."

After a careless shrug, she glided to the desk and rested her hip against it. "I understood you'd taken care of that."

He clamped his eyes shut and muttered a string of multilingual curses. The crystal ball in the corner caught his attention, the gray mist within swirling around like a tempest in the storm. How much had she seen of his visit in the telling orb?

She laughed. "That's your problem, Chairman. You can't control everything. You can't control what's happening inside you."

His jaw hurt from the pressure he exerted holding back his furious words, or, worse, spells. It wouldn't do to loose his magick on Sarka. Dark, beautiful, and as powerful as he was, she'd eagerly engage in battle. He had to listen.

"You're like Spock."

"What the fuck are you talking about, Sarka?"

His impatience boiled just beneath the surface. *It won't take much more.*

"Did you ever watch the show? The original?"

He both envied and hated her serene composure. Gritting his teeth, he nodded.

"Like Spock, you see emotion as a weakness. To avoid your empathic ability, you lock it down, never allow it to see the light of day. You spit at the gods when you do that, you know."

He shifted his feet, irritation flooding him. He hated having to stand and listen to this drivel. He needed help. Not a fucking psychoanalytic comparison to a TV character.

"You know, Spock was half human and half Vulcan. Like Myrddin in the legend who was sired by a demon and human woman." Her eyes narrowed. "Is that what you're afraid of, Ian? Letting your emotions out to play will turn you evil?"

Reality punched him in the gut. He hated she had to show him the truth.

"Yes, I'm fucking terrified of how furious I am, how crippled I was when those bastards attacked my son. My son! I want to kill them. Every fucking one of them!" he yelled, unable to lower his voice. Like poison, it burned his throat as the words spilled forth. "They planned to use him to hurt the Syndicate. They attacked Cassidy, killed innocent women and children. They wanted Rekkus's babies. Dana.... They would've killed Dana."

He rambled. He could no more stop his words from tumbling from his mouth than he could stop the world from spinning. His body trembled, his muscles clenched tightly to keep from falling apart.

"I couldn't put her in danger...."

Becca's face flashed in his mind. A fist grasped his heart and squeezed. He gasped at the pain, true and fierce. He pressed his hands to his chest, bending over with the agony.

A cool hand guided him to a chair where he sank into its cushion. Sarka, not known for her kindness and compassion, had given it when he'd needed it.

He took a couple of steadying breaths, the pain in his heart still throbbing. He glanced at her, now calmly pouring a cup of tea near the window. She sipped slowly then carefully placed the china cup on its saucer. She stood in front of the cupboard where it sat, her feet planted apart and her arms at her sides.

A frisson of suspicion sped up his spine.

"You need Becca."

"No!" He shot out of the chair and bellowed the word. "No."

The house shook from the ferocity of his denial, but Sarka stood her ground. "She's your mate. Your intended." Her voice rose with the increased vibration in the room.

"No." He threw his hands out in front of him, stunned when a gust of wind pushed Sarka back a step. She retook her ground, face hard.

"And you're part of her. She came to find who she was. She found you, may the gods help her." Her words thundered above the gusts and rumbling of the floor.

He stared at Sarka, her black hair swirling in the wind.

All the frustration, all the fear, all the rage

exploded. Lightning sparked from his fingertips, the air crackling with his power encircling him like a tornado. Books flew off shelves, ceramic crashed against walls, papers tossed about like autumn leaves.

How could he be so powerful and so helpless? He could no longer contain the ticking time bomb.

"Aah!" With a warrior's cry he threw his arms up toward the ceiling, blowing a hole in the roof with a shower of sparks. The explosion rocked the building, but the walls of Sarka's office stood as did she with her signature smirk on her seemingly unperturbed face.

Ian collapsed to the floor, shaking and spent. He rolled to his back and saw the huge breach in the roof caused by his lack of control.

A pounding on the door caught his attention, and he winced at the destruction he'd caused: books, broken figurines, and papers lay strewn about the floor.

"No, Cemil. I'm fine. Really. The chairman just needed to vent a bit. I'm sure he'll see to the repairs."

How can she be so fucking calm?

The door closed with a click, and she came to stand over him, staring down at him like he was some oddity.

"Is anyone hurt? Is there much damage?" He cringed at the thought of hurting anyone.

"No, the destruction is restricted to this room." She glanced about the room, clucking her tongue as if he'd thrown paper balls instead of real items. "I should have chosen a different spot for you to throw your tantrum."

"What?" Ian jumped to his feet.

She smoothed an errant lock back into place. "You're acting like a child."

With one hand palm out, she stopped his reply. She directed him to sit with an imperious tilt of her head toward a chair, then she took her own behind her desk. He felt like a boy in the principal's office.

"Ian, the fates provided you with what you need to be happy and healthy. You rejected it. It's not what you want. It's not what you asked for. Doesn't that sound like a child reacting to an unwanted, but still precious, present?"

Drained from his emotional outburst, he could not ignore her words. He could not discount the wisdom and truth of her comparison. No longer able to deny the longing in his heart and the cry of his soul for his mate. The weight of casting the spell on Becca hung about his shoulders like an iron yoke.

Energy sent out to the world returned threefold. The fucking spell he'd cast to make her forget him and allow him to obtain the scroll certainly kicked his ass. Defeated, he lowered his head to his hands.

"Now, before you get all emotional on me again, let me suggest a way to reverse your spell." Sarka held out her open palm over the desk. "I need the ruby ring you took from her."

How does she know about the ring?

"Just give it to me."

Her impatience had returned. This was the Sarka he knew and respected, full of snark and sass. He pulled the ring from his pinky finger and placed it in her hand.

"And your ring."

He hesitated. "This is a ring handed down through my family. It belonged to Myrddin."

She simply raised an eyebrow. Obviously she expected him to comply.

"I hope you know what you're doing."

Giving up the ring was hard, but he had to trust in Sarka and the fates. With the twist of her mouth, she plucked it from his outstretched palm and moved to the altar set up against a wall.

He sank back in the cushions, praying to the gods to watch over Becca, to forgive him for distrusting their wisdom. With his eyes closed, Sarka's chants washed over him. The acrid smoke burned his nostrils. He trusted her alchemy.

He opened his eyes when the swish of her skirts approached. Her eyes glowed black, and she wiped sweat from her brow. From the genuine smile on her face, she enjoyed her work. She patted his shoulder and said, "Pour yourself some tea. This may take a while. To paraphrase one of my favorite movies, you can't rush magick. You rush magick, Chairman, you get rotten magick."

Ian accepted her offer and, with a cup of tea, settled into a chair to observe a master at work.

He blinked away sleep from his eyes. How long had he been out? The room was dark save a single lamp burning on Sarka's huge desk. *Damn woman, did she drug me with the tea or cast a sleeping spell?*

In the pool of light thrown from the lamp, a single silver filigree ring with a bloodstone rested on a folded piece of paper.

Stretching his weary muscles as he rose to his

feet, he sighed in resignation. What had Sarka done while he slept? Had she left him a solution or a note mocking his manhood? He deserved no better, but he prayed she'd found compassion in her heart for him.

The ring glittered in the light and warmed his palm. His hand trembled as he picked up the note and unfolded it. The spell written in her aggressive slanted script filled the paper along with a personal message.

Chairman, I witnessed your pathetic marriage proposal to Cassidy Sinclair. I thought you an idiot. I envied you the perfect relationship you found with Ms. Jones, but you confirmed my prior judgment of your character by your most recent actions. Take my help and advice by adhering to the spell exactly as it is written. Don't be an asshat.

***

Becca couldn't shake the uneasy feeling she was missing something. Like going to the kitchen for something and being unable to remember why.

Pushing food around on her plate, she pretended to eat but couldn't stomach food. Trixie sweetly sat with her. She wasn't very good company, though Trixie hadn't left her side all day. Since dinner attendance was required, she'd accompanied the yoga instructor to the dining room.

She barely remembered coming to Wiccan Haus, and the only person she recalled from five days was Trixie. Cyrus Rowan, the tall, dark, and sexy sibling owner of the resort, seemed familiar and acted as if he knew her. At the edges of her mind, a scene in the library where she'd met him and he'd removed his glove to shake her hand.... The memory teased her then faded like morning fog.

Her entire brain seemed fuzzy. There were things she could not pull up, like deleted files that still took up space on her hard drive. She fought the anxiety that something terrible had happened to her in the last several days and someone had erased her memory to keep her sane.

God help me. Despair crowded into her belly and up her throat, burning it. *What is happening to me?*

Cyrus approached, his hard face curving into a warm smile. *Why does he wear gloves?* She bit back the question, not wanting to offend him. She offered him a halfhearted grin.

"Hello, Trixie, Becca. How are you?" It seemed like a loaded question, as if he knew exactly what was wrong.

"Fine."

He firmed his mouth into a line. He'd clearly wanted an honest answer. Why?

"How about a walk after dinner?"

"Isn't it dangerous to walk the grounds at night?" Where did that come from? She'd never walked the trails at night, nor during the day from her recollection. How would she know such information?

Cyrus studied her face. "My dear Becca, you'll be completely safe with me."

Becca glanced at Trixie. "Will you come with us?"

She hated feeling helpless, vacant.

"I think we're done. Let's go." Trixie's statement confirmed she'd noticed Becca rearranging her food.

Cyrus held Becca's chair as she slid out of it. Suspicion crept in. Where were they going?

He followed her out, with Trixie trailing behind them. His hand settled on the small of her back, but no butterflies fluttered in her belly. Why not? Cyrus embodied tall, dark, and sexy.

Myron flipped cards rhythmically on the front desk as they passed through the foyer. She nodded to them and winked at Cyrus. Not flirty. Conspiratorial.

"Where are we going?"

"For a walk, darling. Down to the beach." He paused, facing her, as if waiting for a reaction.

She shivered. "Have there been attacks here, on this path?"

Again, wavering images of a huge wolf frozen in midair, of a man she'd seen earlier in the day and maybe on the ferry shimmered in her mind, just out of reach. She squeezed her eyes shut, trying to focus all her energy on grabbing the elusive memory. She fisted her hands at her sides in her effort.

"She's remembering." Trixie's whisper drew her out of her concentration.

"Remembering what?"

Cyrus's hand on her back kept her moving forward. Toward what, she didn't know.

"Trust me, Becca. I'll make sure you are safe." His voice resonated honesty. Instinctively, she trusted him.

The path turned. She gasped at the sheer

beauty of the beach below her and the full moon seemingly within her reach. A fire burned, silhouetting the form of a man. From the bluff, she couldn't make out his identity, but this scenario seemed hauntingly familiar. She'd experienced déjà vu before but *knew* she'd been here during the last few days.

Cyrus assisted her down the steep path leading to the cove. Trixie's footfalls followed them.

"I've been here before," Becca said, struggling to grab the fleeting images only to have them unravel at the edges and slip away. As they neared the man by the fire, his features became clear. His soft green eyes and those firm lips currently set in a determined line—she knew them but his name escaped her. She'd run her hands through his silver-tipped dark brown hair and from the sharp electric response of her body, he'd inspired and fulfilled fantasies she couldn't remember.

Cyrus and Trixie remained silent, but they knew something. This secrecy frustrated her.

This is my life. I can't remember the last four days and I need answers. Now.

She ground her teeth against the urge to scream.

Ian. His name is Ian. How could she know this?

Cyrus stopped a few feet from Ian. The firelight revealed his taut jaw and a muscle jumping there.

Whatever Ian was doing, Cyrus had some reservations.

"She's remembering. It's all or nothing, Chairman. Don't screw up."

A clear warning, but about what?

Ian nodded. "No, you're right, Cyrus. It's all."

"She's stronger than you think."

"I know."

"No. I mean her powers come from the same source as yours. That's why she's breaking the spell on her own."

"I'm right here, you know."

Staying quiet to acquire information was one thing, having them talk about her as if she weren't there was quite another. She skewered Ian with a glare. "You. Tell me what the hell is going on or I swear to God, I'll kick your ass."

Cyrus snickered beside her and she slapped at his arm. "Shut up!"

A strange charge ran up her arm from where her fingertips had briefly touched Cyrus. A quick couple of frames flashed in her mind. Gloves, bare hand, documents. Jolting, painful visions of the past.

She turned, reached up, and placed her palm on his whisker-roughened cheek. His eyes held such pain. Cyrus remained perfectly still, seeming to know she needed to understand what was happening. How did she know he fought with sorrow and had dealt with incredible, crippling loss?

A surge of anger rocked her physically. She glanced at Trixie. Maybe, Cyrus was her man or desired him. Trixie's aura of serenity made her dismiss the possibility.

Wait. Aura? What the hell?

She swayed again with a second wave of emotion. To keep her balance, she dropped her hand from Cyrus's face while he reached out to steady her. The anger tightened to a burning ball in her belly.

A sharp inhale from Ian drew her attention. His nostrils flared as he stared at Cyrus's hand on her upper arm.

Not anger. Jealousy. Well, fuck him. He doesn't own me. In fact, if he has anything to do with this memory loss, I don't ever want to see him again.

His expression changed instantly from scowling to trepidation.

I'm sorry.

How can I hear his thoughts?

Because I love you.

Fuck you. If you loved me, you wouldn't have done this.

I did it because I love you.

The truth of his words and his stormy emotions overwhelmed her. Tears slid down her cheeks.

"All of you know what is going on. Enlighten me. Something important was being kept from her and, damn it, she needed to know.

Trixie cleared her throat. "Becca." Her calmness irritated. "The only way to discover the whole truth is to allow Ian to cast a spell."

"What? That's it, isn't it? He cast a spell on me to make me forget." Becca backed away from Ian until she bumped against Cyrus's warm chest. Immediately, Ian's jealousy pulsed hot. "Screw you, Ian. I don't care if you're jealous. Or mad. Or sorry."

Becca turned to Trixie. "Why should I let him do his hocus pocus on me again?"

Trixie moved to where she stood in the protection of Cyrus's presence. She placed her hand on Becca's arm. "Breathe in and let your mind free. See what I have seen. Then you can make an informed decision."

Why not? It's all in my imagination, anyway. I'm probably cuckoo for Cocoa Puffs. Becca closed her eyes, breathed in and out, slowly relaxing her tension and opening her mind to possibilities.

A slideshow of images played in her mind. Yoga with cranky Ian. Breakfast with smiling Ian. A walk, hand-in-hand, by the waterfall with Ian. From Trixie's point of view, they were happy, in love.

In love.

Oh God. Her mind tried to will it away, but she couldn't deny the utter agony crushing her chest, burning in her throat, leaking from her eyes.

I love him.

His eyebrows drew together, and the corners of his mouth dragged down. Clearly, he shared her pain.

Cyrus's arms banded around her and kept her from sliding to the ground. Trixie's voice broke through a cacophony of returning memories.

"Breathe, Becca. In, one, two, three, four. Out, one, two, three, four. You, too, Ian. You have to be strong for her now. She was there for you. It's your turn." Her voice turned sharp. "Do it! Now."

Instantly, the pain lessened by half. *Ahh, Ian's pain. He's hurting, too. Good. Stupid fucking sorcerer.*

Sorcerer. Myrddin, the historical predecessor of the Merlin legend. Ian descended from Myrddin.

The last day, the last moments, cleared in her fuzzy mind. This beach. The scroll. The spell revealing Myrddin's lost lover, his child in her

89

womb. He'd sent her away like Ian had planned.

They'd come together there, too. Their souls had mated, he'd called it. And then he'd said a few words. Those words must have removed her memory of him and Myrddin as her own ancestor.

"Why?"

Still pained that she stood with Cyrus, Ian firmed his mouth and admitted the truth. "I thought it was safer for you, Becca. Paranormals have enemies, ones who would capture and torture you to do their bidding. Or kill you to get to me. If you were with me."

She stepped away from Cyrus and looked up at him. "That's what happened to you?"

"Half my family was slaughtered to get to me." His voice never wavered, but his pain radiated from him in needle-sharp pulses. She glanced at his gloved hands. "I'm a retrocog. I can read an object's history by touch."

She did not fully understand his power. He obviously valued his privacy and had provided all she needed to know right now.

Trixie shrugged with a rueful grin. "I'm just an intuitive human. No powers."

Becca returned her grin. "I'm not sure about that, Trix. You're more than you seem."

Ian's anxiety pulsed through her. It was strange but thrilling to experience another person's feelings. Time to deal with him.

Striding to Ian with a renewed sense of needing closure—or was it a new beginning—Becca stopped inches from his face. Hope pounded through her. His or hers?

"Do the spell." No matter what, Becca needed

answers, now.

A cautiously grateful smile curved his lips while he scrutinized her face. Was he reading emotions like she was doing with him? If they descended from the same wizard, did she have the same innate abilities, but dormant? And what about their relationship? Could it be salvaged?

Could he ever make it up to her?

Ian's heart clenched painfully with each beat. She remembered almost everything and now it appeared the time to give her everything else—her heritage and his complete heart and soul. He'd shared his soul with her but not his confidence, not his fears. He'd never fully trusted, allowed someone else in. Now, he had to lay himself bare to her in front of witnesses.

So be it.

He dragged a hand through his hair, yanking and using the pain to center himself. He forced his gaze to hers. She was so damn beautiful when she was furious. Later, he prayed, she'd give him the chance to show her she meant the world to him.

"Take this."

With his palm out, he offered Becca the ring Sarka had created for him. "Put it on and I'll say the spell." Imminently grateful that she took it and ecstatic that she placed it on the ring finger of her left hand, Ian shot a look at Cyrus. The imposing Rowan raised an eyebrow as if to say, *Don't mess this up or you'll deal with me.* Becca inspired a man's protective instincts, and he could tell Cyrus appreciated her sweet spirit and honest passion. The man would gladly step into his place if she rejected him as her mate. Ian didn't blame him.

Once he unfolded Sarka's spell, he took a cleansing breath.

Please, Myrddin, if you ever grant me one wish, help me unravel this unholy mess I've made with Becca.

Protect my legacy....

How do I protect your legacy and my sanity? He blew out a deep sigh. *I'm sorry, Myrddin.*

With the paper in one hand, he reached out to clasp her hand with the other. His heart dropped at her apprehension in giving him her left hand, the one with the ring. He had no other choice. Becca Jones was his other half and without her he had no balance. He would be broken and ineffective to protect anyone, especially his son. And Becca.

A deep breath and a silent prayer later, he intoned Sarka's spell in Welsh.

O ffynnon o bŵer (From the fountain of power)

Tynnaf fy hud (I draw my magick)

O waed Myrddin (From Myrddin's blood)

Yr wyf yn eu geni (I am born)

Yr wyf yn galw ar ein gwaed (I call on our blood)

I adfer hyn a gymerwyd (To restore what was taken)

Ian dropped the paper to the ground.

I shouldn't ask. Yes, I need all the help I can get. He added his own line to the spell.

Adfer ei chariad i mi (Restore her love for me)

Wind circled, sealing them in the updraft.

Becca's hair gleamed like fire as it was drawn skyward. Her wide eyes showed no fear, only wonder. She reached out her free hand to touch the funneling wind, and giggled. The wider her smile grew, the lighter his heart became. Hope emerged like the first crocus after a long, hard winter.

Tender hope withered when she drew her left hand from his and stared at the ring Sarka forged. Becca twirled it on her finger, narrowing her eyes as she examined it.

"Mae hyn yn fy, eto nid pwll." *This is mine, yet not mine.*

He understood the words, yet she'd uttered them in Welsh. His mind searched the wording of the spell.

By the gods, Sarka had tricked him. *Damn her, this wasn't her decision to make.*

The line he'd read had said "Restore what was taken." All the missing pieces of her parent's past lay at her feet. Once the puzzle was fully assembled, she'd have access to her father's power.

Am I ready for that? Is she?

The choice was no longer his. The spark in her eyes from her blood's memory supplied the answers she'd searched for since she was old enough to understand she had no father.

In the spiraling wind she was like a phoenix rising—frightening and awe-inspiring. With her newfound power, she might not want him, might resent him for stealing her heritage from her. Love might not be enough; he'd broken her trust.

She took his breath away. And he'd be damned if he didn't do everything in his considerable power to make her his again.

Protect my legacy....
Sorry, Myrddin—
Wait. A cold shiver ran up his spine. *I am as big an idiot as Sarka thinks I am.*

Becca's glowing face, her radiant smile as she played her fingers through the now sparkling wind stream—intuitively, she'd sent a trail of golden sparks winding into the funnel—cemented his realization. Myrddin's legacy was Becca. She was of the blood, as was he.

The great wizard had been trying to tell him to break the legacy of loneliness, of loveless sacrifice, to protect humanity and paranormal kind. Many generations separated them, but he—and probably Becca's father—had sacrificed happiness for their part in maintaining peace and harmony. His ancestor wanted his family reunited, desired balance for his children.

He no longer had to choose. He could fulfill his obligations to protect his kind and have his all-consuming love.

If she gave him the chance.

After inhaling for courage, he stepped closer and cupped her face. Her forest-green eyes reflected the glittery wind tunnel before she focused on him. For a moment, his heart stopped. *Take me, all my flaws, all my faults, for I love you with all that I am.*

A smile tugged at one corner of her mouth, and his heart pumped again.

I love you, Ian, for the idiot Sarka thinks you are. For all your flaws and faults, I love you. Now, take me home or lose me forever.

He crushed his mouth to hers, intensely

grateful when she returned every bit of the passion he poured into the kiss. With one arm wrapped around her, he muttered, "Hold on."

She tightened the grip she already had around his shoulders but never pulled back. Her lips never left his.

With a flick of his wrist, they were standing in his room.

She pulled back and smiled sweetly up at him. "I love you, Ian, but if you ever do anything like that again, I will castrate you."

Involuntarily, he placed a hand over his family jewels and nodded. She would soon be every bit as powerful as he was, and, even without powers, a woman scorned was to be feared.

"Yes, dear."

With a cocky grin, she began unbuttoning her blouse. "Now, I sense you've missed me. Show me how much."

The member she'd threatened a moment ago throbbed painfully.

"Whatever you wish, *fy nghariad*."

"I wish for you."

"Done."

With a snap, her clothes disappeared, and she stood gloriously naked before him. She raised her eyebrows and raked him head to toe with her gaze.

"A little overdressed for this event, aren't you?"

Confident and curvaceous, the woman who completed him, who reined in his emotions and set him free all at once, was his, just as most assuredly he was hers.

Sometimes, magick facilitated. He snapped his fingers again, and, as she scorched his now bared skin with lust in her eyes, she licked her lips. Electricity zapped every thought as he focused on her tongue.

"Ian?"

"Huh?" Had she spoken? She didn't need to. Now they were together; they need only think to communicate.

Fine. Did you miss me?

He had her beneath him, her lips opening to his marauding mouth, her fingers digging into his back. She met his every nibble with a nip and every slide of his tongue with her own.

Skin to skin, he trembled at her power over him. She moaned as his mouth traveled along her cheek to her jaw. His body surged against hers, impressing upon her his urgency.

His hands slid everywhere, reacquainting him with the woman he'd thought lost to him. She gasped as he stroked one nipple then the other. His own breath caught as she moved her hand between their bodies to wrap her fingers around his painfully engorged shaft.

Becca....

Touch me.

He pushed up on his elbow and gazed into her eyes. "I love you."

"I know. I love you, too." Her small smile morphed to a gasp as he slid a finger into her heat.

"You wanted me to show you how much I've missed you?"

He stroked out, then in again. She gasped again but kept her gaze on him. She barely nodded, but her eyes widened as he pushed her knees apart to position himself between them.

Gently he eased into her until his chest rested lightly on hers. Face-to-face, he nibbled at her lips and murmured, "This is going to be a wild ride."

"Good."

He jolted into her when she sucked his lower lip into her mouth. He lost any thread of control he'd ever had with her and bucked into her. She raised her hips, met his thrusts—every one—all the while staring into his eyes.

He swore a star went nova there before her eyes squeezed shut and she screamed his name. How many times, he didn't know, and, to his shame, didn't care. Blood drummed in his temples, obliterating all other sound. Sweat dribbled down his back, his nose, his chest. The ever-tightening coil in his loins exploded. A groan broke from its constraints in his lungs, echoing on the walls.

Frozen for a moment, every nerve firing in mass chaos, Ian drew air into his lungs then forced it out again. Tension drained out of him, all those bunched muscles relaxing at once. He eased to one side, remaining encased in her sweet, still-pulsing body, and nuzzled his face into the crook of her neck.

"Are you okay? I was a bit rough."

A sigh caressed his neck, followed by her hand stroking his hair.

"Ian, I am your match. The only way you can hurt me is by leaving. Or turning your back on me."

No matter what, he'd never make such a mistake again. He'd help locate her father, dead or alive, fulfill whatever dreams she had. He couldn't wait to introduce her to Allan, weave together their lives. With her at his side, his power and strength would grow.

He recalled the vision of Myrddin turning his pregnant lover away. He blinked, only now a smiling Myrddin embraced Anwyn with one arm and held a swaddled red-haired baby in his other. He'd never seen his forefather smile in any dream or vision before. He—Ian—had fulfilled Myrddin's dream and his own.

"No chance of that happening, *fy nghariad.* I am only a fool once."

About the Author

Carolyn Spear was raised in a rural Tidewater Virginia, the kind of place where everyone knows everyone. While she's moved around the Eastern Seaboard, she's back home in Tidewater, married with two teenage girls and a pampered princess of a dog.

As a teenager, she sneaked her mother's Barbara Cartland romances. These historical romances full of dashing British rogues and spirited ingenues opened a door to another world. Now, years later, Carolyn's mission is to introduce readers to her world.

For more about Carolyn and her works-in-progress, visit http://www.carolynspearromance.com/